I0745758

White Moccasins

THE STORY OF KATIE

White Moccasins

THE STORY OF KATIE

Sandra Lee Cleary

FRANKLIN
SCRIBES™
PUBLISHERS

Library of Congress Control Number: 2016902673
An Historical Fiction
ISBN 9781941516126
First Edition

Published by Franklin Scribes Publishers
Franklin Scribes is a registered trademark of Franklin Scribes Publishers
Cibolo, Texas
Email: franklinscribeswrites@gmail.com

To contact the author, email Sandraleecleary@gmail.com
Visit her blog at journeythroughourbranches.com

Library of Congress Control Number: 2016902673
ISBN 9781941516126

Newspaper Article Credits:
The Dubuque Times, Dubuque, Iowa
Saturday Evening, Jan 8, 1892
Cover photo credits: Jennifer Bowman
Editor: Brenda Blanchard
Cover design: Jennifer Bowman
Katie portrayed by Aubree Bowman

Acknowledgments

I praise my Lord and Savior for showing me patience and perseverance. Thank you. To my family who stood by me even though I shooed them away from my office door to work franticly on this book. To my husband, Curtis, for his support and let it be known he has the patience of a saint. To my children Steve, Angel, Raylene, Jennifer, Kathy, and Joe and to my many grandchildren and great grandchildren. To all of my friends who have waited so patiently for me to finally put the last period in place. Thank you.

To my critique group, the Christian Writers Group of San Antonio. I couldn't have done it without your input and encouragement. Thank you to my editor Brenda Blanchard whose reassuring words kept telling me I needed to write. She saw something I didn't. Thank you.

Most of all, thank you to my dearest friend and business partner, Judy Watters, for your inspiration, critiquing, and editing. Thank you.

Last but not least to Judy Buss and Celia Wyburn who took the DNA tests for me. I really thought we were related at one point. That's the next book. I'm proud to say we have become very close friends through this work of love. You both are great, great, great, granddaughters of Katies. I pray I've done her story justice. Thank you.

It took a village to keep me on track. Thank you.

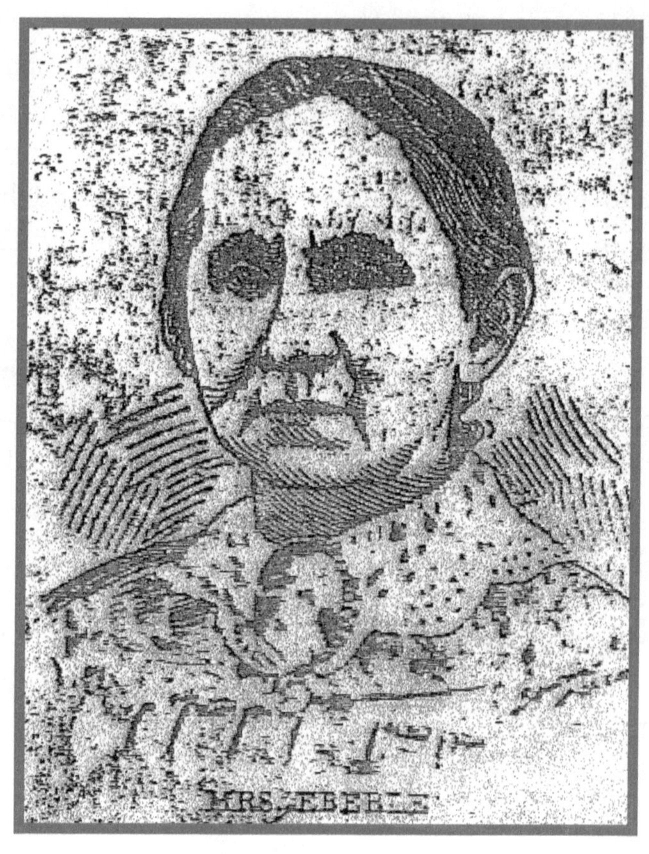

Catherine Jordan Eberle

"Katie"

Abt. 1892

Chapter 1

Dubuque, Iowa 1916

Long forgotten memories came flooding back as I stood watching the bulldozer tear down the eighty-five year old log cabin where my grandmother once lived. The carefully chiseled logs had settled and the mud between the logs had long ago chipped away. Two cloudy windows framed the old wooden door that hung lopsided on one hinge. Why the door hadn't fallen off before now remained a mystery. It reminded me of someone who kept waiting for a reprieve, hoping someone would come along to mend it. I heard somewhere that the windows came all the way from St. Louis by way of a keelboat making its way up the Mississippi.

If walls could only talk, they'd speak of rich history, the laughter and tears. Each board had heard the words of fear from another Indian uprising. Of Grandmother Katie learning the white man's language and ways when the Jordan family took her in after the massacre. Then, there was Samuel's and Father Jordan's deaths.

The city council had talked of moving the cabin to a museum site, but in the end, the city said to tear it down. Like so many other cities, make way for the new.

I watched as cameras flashed, bobbing up and down as reporters clambered, pushing each other, to make sure their picture made the front page. Each man flipped through his note pad and jotted details of the last occupant, Katie, a young Indian girl who lived in the same camp as Black Hawk. They listened as the local historian conveyed the story of Indian Kate, the name the white man gave her through their mutual love and respect, of Kate; being rescued by a local family, and how the family raised her as their own.

Tears slid down my cheeks as I remembered the last time I sat in this small two and a half-room cabin listening to my Grandmother Katie telling me stories of her childhood. How she escaped the battle between her people, the Sauk Indians, and the white man. The war known in history books as the Black Hawk War of 1832.

Peering around the doorway, I watched Grandmother sitting at her small dressing table staring in the mirror. It was as if she were remembering something. A winsome smile crossed her deep-lined face as she smoothed her black hair back into the knot she wore on the top of her head. Although her eyes spoke of wisdom and her smooth skin had turned to furrowed lines, her hair was still as black as coal. Her eyes became moist and distant.

"Grandma, what are you doing?"

Startled, she dropped something into a box and swung around just as I pounced upon her lap. "My Little Butterfly, I didn't hear you."

"Were you busy, Grandma?"

"No, I was just thinking."

I took her hand in mine and ran my fingers over her calloused fingers and palm. "Thinking of what, Grandma?"

She brushed my unruly hair back away from my face. "I was thinking of my mother, Little Butterfly."

"What was her name?"

"Kat-e-quah."

I giggled. "Grandma, that sounds like Katie."

She had that same faraway look. "It does sound a lot like Katie."

"Is that why my name is Katie?"

She smiled, gave me a hug, and kissed the top of my head. She pulled my hair back behind my ears. "That is why your name is Katie, just like mine, Little Butterfly."

Grandma stood up and took my hand. She led me to her rocker in the corner of the cabin, next to the fireplace and lifted me onto her lap. We began rocking. I felt warm all over when Grandma rocked me and held me tight. I settled into Grandma's tender embrace and breathed in the sweet fragrance of honeysuckle in her hair that I remember to this day. She began her story.

Chapter 2

May 1832

With snows melting, we made our way back from the hunting grounds to our summer camp along the great river. Black Hawk said it was time for the women to plant their crops. But, there was turmoil ever since we returned.

On our arrival, Black Hawk and many braves found our lodges occupied with white men. One night I stood by our wigwam and listened as Black Hawk spoke to our braves about the white man taking our land. Although I could not hear everything, I heard Black Hawk's voice over the din of the crowd.

"White men claims he has bought this land. I tell him this land cannot be sold, it belongs to the Great Spirit."

A few days later, Black Hawk, along with a handful of braves, his friend Elijah, a soldier adopted by the Sauk, and two squaws went to Fort Armstrong to hear the demands of the soldiers. "I say this to the white chief that Black Hawk would have been a friend to the pale face, but they would not let him—the hatchet was dug up by themselves not by the Indians. I would have gone back across the Mississippi but when the white flag was raised one of my warriors was shot. Now, Black Hawk will have revenge until the Great

Spirit shall say to him, come away. Provoke our people to war, and you will know who Black Hawk is."

With that said, Black Hawk turned and walked out of the council with our women and warriors following behind him.

After that meeting with the white man, Black Hawk held war games with each brave fighting against another. Many of the women and young girls watched as the braves fought hand-to-hand with knives. Our chief drilled the braves with tomahawks and guns until they were ready to fight.

Black Hawk was of small stature but stood erect and straight, with a broad chest and a splendid physique. His thin lips spoke words of truth. He moved with the grace of a mountain lion. Upon his head he proudly displayed his bright red headdress made of colored deer fur and porcupine hair, but not the sharp quills of the porcupine. Many braves and chiefs from other tribes respected his wisdom and listened to what he had to say. Black Hawk, renowned as a great warrior with exceptional intelligence, led his people to many victories. I had not seen such fighting before, but by the looks of things, and what I heard my parents say about previous battles, this battle would be no different.

When not hunting or fighting, Black Hawk sat with the elders at night around the fire talking. I heard him tell the elders, as they smoked and passed his pipe around the circle, that they were once as happy as the buffalo on the plains, now they were as miserable as the hungry, howling wolf on the prairie. My father said Black Hawk was a family man devoted and true to his wife and children. He called Black Hawk straight forward, a man of character, and of great courage. With his braves, they won many battles.

Mother said he had a quiet strength about him. At times when Black Hawk came into camp after hunting all day, the women would giggle. They stared at him in a funny way. I overheard Mother say to other women of the camp that he was manly. I didn't know what that meant, but her words made the women snort.

After his last return from the fort, Black Hawk took the horses with our women and children, and told the men we had to leave. "We have fought many battles before, but this time there will be great fighting. We must leave this place and go to higher ground to make our stand."

Chapter 3

August 1832

This story is not easy to tell. Many things have happened between my people and the white people. Things like land grabbing, killing, and hatred of each other because of the color of their skin, but it's a story that needs to be told.

Though many years have passed, when everything feels calm and quiet, I can still hear the screams of my people. I was all of seven years old then, your age, Little Butterfly. It was a quiet evening; we'd been traveling all day, and we were tired. A long trip with children riding horses while other horses carried our big packs. The horses carried us through swamps, up hills and down, around and through trees, until you'd think we'd all fall off our mounts. I grew so tired and hungry, but I knew not to complain. If I complained, it meant I didn't deserve the safety of the Great Spirit.

Of course, not one of us children thought we were in any danger. To us, it seemed like we were moving our camp as we had done so many times in the past.

It was late afternoon, just as the sun topped the trees to begin its retreat for the evening. The women had finished putting our wigwams together. I helped my sisters add weeds and grass to our puckway around the wigwam. This kept out the chilly winds that blew across the river. My father along with my brother, Kenwikomata, hunted on the ridge surrounding our camp. A few warriors stayed behind to guard the camp. When I finished with the puckway, I went to help Mother as she showed me how to turn the rabbit above the fire.

"It's time you learn how to cook like your sisters."

My little brother, Sionoh, played with other boys taking their sticks and hitting the ball nearby.

My head jerked up as shots rang out. I dropped the rabbit in the fire when I saw soldiers in their dark, gray uniforms galloping into our camp shouting, firing guns and flaying their long knives. The air filled with smoke from gunfire mixed with the aroma of our rabbit cooking. There were too many soldiers to count. I covered my eyes to shield the glare of their brass buckles shining in the setting sun. I reached for Sionoh's arm, but he pulled free and ran toward Mother.

Loud bursts filled the air and dirt flew everywhere. I stood frozen and watched as friends fell from a shower of flying objects. One of the pieces landed next to me. In my terror, I knelt down to take a better look. All sound around me was gone as I picked it up; I turned it over and over in my hands. It looked like a big piece of round lead from the mines. Then again, it looked like a large piece of flint stone our braves used for their arrows. Someone ran past me and knocked me down. The noise of rifles firing, my people wailing and screaming, and the braves' war whoops hurt my ears. I put my hands over them to block out the sounds. From the ground, I watched white men take the scalps of some of my people. I had to help my family.

In the distance, I saw Black Hawk and his men on the

ridge charging toward our camp throwing their tomahawks and knives. Women ran to gather their children. I heard my mother yell to my sister, "Take Memekeha and run."

Anomosa grabbed my arm and jerked me off the ground, almost dragging me. She grabbed my blanket beside the wigwam, where I had thrown it down, and threw it at me. "Take this, you may need it."

The crack of gunfire echoed in my ears, and a strong charcoal odor filled my nostrils. The horses' pounding hooves thundered behind me as my sister dragged me into the tall grass. "Come on Memekeha, or you will die, too."

I tore my arm from my sister and headed back toward our wigwam to help my mother. She needed my help; so did my little brother. Anomosa grabbed me from behind and turned me around.

"What are you doing? Mother said to run. Let's go."

We started to run but not before I turned again and watched my mother pick up my little brother and run in another direction. Behind her, my aunt and her children followed trying to get out of the way of the horses. Everyone scrambled, picking up children as they ran.

My sister pulled me away. Tears stung my eyes while tall blades of grass struck my face. We ran so fast; my legs couldn't keep up with hers. The elders always said Anamosa ran like the wind. I clutched my pouch to keep it from swaying while I ran.

Mother's words echoed in my head. "Go with Anamosa. Do not look back; run, little one, run!"

How long we ran I did not know. My throat hurt as I gasped for air. We stopped to hide in the bushes not making a sound, but we could still hear the horses' hooves and men yelling.

My sister urged me on toward the river, staying close to the edge ducking in and out of the brush. Then Anamosa saw a canoe close to shore. We crawled through the brush out to the canoe, and she helped me over the side.

"Where are we going?" I asked. I didn't want to get too far away from Mother and Father.

She put her finger to her lips to signal silence while she shook her head back and forth. She pushed our canoe out into the current where it was carried quickly down river. We were at the mercy of the river with no paddle to help guide us.

I covered my ears with my hands again to drown out the fading sounds of gunfire and the screams that sliced the air. Soon trees along the shore loomed in the darkness throwing mysterious shadows against the water.

The current carried our canoe toward the island in the middle of the river. I turned around to see flames reaching higher and higher into the sky--like the cries of my people calling out to the Great Spirit. The flames soared, licking the cold dark sky.

My sister pushed my head down into the canoe so I couldn't see. I felt the cool water through the floor of the canoe, and heard it swirl around and lap at the sides of the canoe. We hit the sandbar with a thud. The canoe tipped over as we both tried to get out at the same time, sending us into the cold water.

I grabbed my blanket and splashed and thrashed trying to keep my head above water. I thought I'd die just like the times mother plunged me into the water trying to make me learn to swim. Mother got upset with me, grabbed me by my hair, and pulled me back into our canoe. This time, my sister dragged me to shore. Tired and exhausted, we laid on the ground trying to catch our breath. I clutched my blanket.

Anamosa found a dry place for us in the thick brush along the shore. "We'll stay here for the night. In the morning, we can go back to our village."

My sister's arms held me tight, and I pressed closer to her for warmth. The many sounds of the night that quieted me when I slept near my parents, now made me shiver with fright. Anamosa placed my wet blanket at my feet. "It will dry by morning," she said.

The smell of smoke still lingered in the air as I lay there next to my sister. It was quiet. No gunfire or screams of my people. Too quiet. I clutched my sister's dress and drew nearer to her. I wondered where Mother, Father, and my little brother slept tonight.

Chapter 4

August 2, 1832

I must have dozed off. Something startled me. From the glow of the small crescent-shaped moon, I could almost see my sister's face as she crouched over me. She felt my blanket to test its wetness and decided against wrapping me in it.

"Memekeha, lie back down next to your blanket, it's still too damp for you to lie on right now. Don't make a sound. Remember what Mother taught us when there is danger. Lie still."

I grabbed her arm. "Where are you going?" I whispered.

"I'll be right back." She peeled my hands from her arm. "Do not move!" She pulled up some tall grass and laid it over me to shield me from the late summer chill. "This will help keep you warm until I get back."

Mother always said I was a good girl. I did as I was told and always helped. Even now, I wouldn't want her to be ashamed of me. I tried to get comfortable; with my head on my arm, I played with the fur on my blanket. I was cold and I started to shiver.

Even though my new blanket was pretty, it felt clammy next to my skin. Mother spent many hours during our winter camp weaving beads onto the edges of the fur then painting the sun and our wigwam on the other side. She made my new blanket from a piece of buffalo hide too small for her or Father. Each night, she made sure to wrap me securely in it when I went to sleep. I felt safe when Mother wrapped me. I felt protected knowing my parents slept only a few feet from me. Tonight was different with grass over me. I clutched the end of my wet blanket next to me. I worried and wanted to know where my parents were. *Were they looking for me?*

The soldiers swooped into our camp before we had eaten our evening meal. I was hungry. My growling stomach was loud enough for a bear, or a coyote, or a wolf to hear. Despite the rumbling in my stomach, exhaustion overtook me, my eyes closed, and I fell into a deep sleep.

• • •

All too soon, the warmth of the sun on my nose made me feel warm all over, and I fought against opening my sluggish eyes. Listening for sounds, I heard nothing. I brushed the grass away and sat up. My arm hurt from being bent under my head all night. I didn't see my sister. *Should I call out to her? What if someone else heard me?* I sat still, waiting to hear something, anything.

Maybe my sister went to look for food. I laid back down on my stomach, looking both to the right and then to the left. I saw no one. I heard not a sound. I softly called out, "Anamosa."

I flinched, as I looked up to see my sister leaning over me with her fingers to her lips. "Hush, Memekeha, someone will hear you. Our canoe is gone, and we must get back across the river."

I grabbed my blanket that had dried in the sun and wrapped it around my shoulders. My legs were wobbly as I slowly stood up. My stomach growled. "I'm hungry."

I stepped out from the brush and stretched.

My sister turned and hurried back to the river's edge. I ran to catch up to her. "I'm hungry."

Irritated with me, she grabbed my hand and jerked me along. "You are always thinking of your stomach. You are not the only one hungry you know. We can eat when we get back to camp." She stopped as suddenly as she started, turned to look at me, and softly said, "Come along, Memekeha, I don't know where Mother or Father are, but I'm sure we'll find them." She brushed my hair back from my eyes. "I'll take care of you until then."

With each step, visions of the day before filled my head. *Did the screams and gunfire really happen or did I wander away from camp and dream it?* Reality hit me when I took a deep breath. I could still smell smoke mixed with something indescribable. Everything was quiet except for the rustle of leaves from a soft breeze.

We made our way to the river and fell down at its edge to get a drink. Cupping my hands, I drank until my stomach hurt.

Anamosa wrenched my arm bringing me upright. "Come on, Memekeha, we will have to swim across the river. Get your blanket and get on my back."

I thought of the last time my mother left me in the water, gasping for air. The water went over my head before my father jumped in to rescue me. Frightened, I looked at Anamosa and pleaded with her. "No, I'm afraid."

She spoke between clenched teeth. "I told you the canoe is gone. Stay here or get on my back."

Reluctantly, I waded out into the cold water with my sister. The sun felt warm on my face. A few feet more, and she placed my arm around her neck, "Put your blanket between us so it stays with us. Hold on and don't let go."

Visions of my mother sitting in the canoe while I struggled in the water haunted me. I was so afraid of the water. *What if I couldn't touch the bottom? I'd sink and drown.* I remembered one afternoon in particular. My mother paddled our canoe out into the river, picked me up, and threw me into the water. Like other mothers, she sat in the canoe and watched to see if I would swim over to the canoe or to the shore. However, she left me in the water too long, and I began thrashing around and crying for help. My father had been away on a hunting trip and came home earlier than expected He saw me in the water, jumped in, and pulled me to shore. My father was so upset with my mother because she just sat in the canoe and watched. He took my mother back to our camp and beat her. That was the last time I had a swimming lesson.

We finally reached the other side and quickly hid behind bushes for safety. Spreading my blanket across the low bushes to dry, we sat nearby watching the river flow.

"I'm hungry."

"Let me rest for a while. Then I'll find you something to eat."

I sat back, crossed my arms, and pouted. Something in the river made me take notice. "Look, what's that floating?"

I focused on the object and a shiver ran through my body. It was a brave floating face down. *Was he from our village? Were there more"*

My sister pushed me, face down, into the bushes. Slimy mud mixed with rocks dug into my palms. "I can't breathe!"

"Hush. Someone is going to hear you. There may be more white men close by."

We lay in the bushes for a long time with my stomach growling louder than before.

After a long time, my sister stood up. "It's quiet; we'd better get going to find our village. Stay behind me."

Again, I did as I was told, too scared to make a noise, not wanting to make her angry. A minute passed. "I'm hungry."

She threw her head back and between clenched teeth again she said, "I know that, Memekeha. I told you, I'll find something."

We walked slowly through the bushes, careful not to make a sound. Anamosa spotted a mulberry bush and stopped to pick a few of the not too ripe berries. She handed them to me. I quickly popped them in my mouth and began to chew. I wrinkled my nose as I ate them, but it filled my stomach for now.

. . .

It seemed like we walked for hours. The smell of burned flesh filled our nostrils before we reached our village. Everything was quiet, no chirping of birds, no barking of dogs, not even the stirring of the leaves. Anamosa peered from behind a tree as she held her arm behind her to keep me from running out into the open. She fell to her knees and pulled me down alongside of her. I stared at the mangled bodies lying on the ground, left from the night before. Short whiffs of wispy smoke from our wigwams fought their way to the sky.

Anamosa took my hand, and we walked closer to where our wigwam had stood.

Careful where I walked, I stopped to take one last look at the smoldering ruins of my home. My foot hit something in the dirt. I bent over to pick it up. I turned it over in my hand and brushed off the dirt.

Anamosa grabbed my hand and jerked me. "I hear something. Quick. We must leave. No one is left here. We have to find out where the rest of our people went."

I tucked the dirty comb into my pouch before my sister saw it. I wanted to keep looking for my mother, but my sister pulled me with her. Maybe Mother escaped. That's it, she escaped and she's waiting for us. We had to keep looking for her, and my brothers and sisters. I know Father is watching over them and keeping them safe. They're probably wondering where we are. I had to believe it.

We walked all afternoon ducking behind bushes when we thought we heard voices. It was early morning when we ate that handful of berries. Now my stomach felt nothing; it wasn't even growling. The sun began to fade below the horizon and once again, the chill of the night filled the air. I couldn't go on. With both feet planted firmly together I stopped. "I'm tired. I'm hungry." I crossed my arms. "Can't we stop?"

Anamosa turned around and glared at me. She put her hands on her hips. "In a little while, I have to find a safe place for us to sleep."

She fell to her knees and drew me to her.

"I know you're tired and hungry, little one. Just a little bit farther."

Once again, she started walking. I heard the weariness in her voice and continued to follow her. My legs felt like they couldn't take another step, but I pushed on afraid she would leave me behind. I dragged my blanket behind me.

"Pick up your blanket, Memekeha."

How does she know I am dragging my blanket? I sat down. "I can't go any more. My legs hurt. I'm tired."

Anamosa didn't even look back. "You're always whining. Do you want the white man to catch you? We must find Mother and Father. Get up, we have to go on."

Reluctantly I got up but sat down again. Anamosa turned around and, for a minute, a look of sorrow filled her eyes. "Oh, I guess we can stay here for the night. Let me brush some of the branches back; then I can wrap you in your blanket. It's finally dried out enough so you won't get chilled." The nest she made of the tall grass looked inviting. She patted the ground for me to join her. "I know you're tired and hungry, but tomorrow will be a better day."

This would be another night away from our people. The sweet smell of the grass tickled my nose. It smelled fresh, like after a summer rain. I wished I had a bowl of boiled corn right then, or maybe even a piece of rabbit that Mother roasted so well. *I wonder if we will find our people tomorrow.* My eyes closed.

Chapter 5

August 3, 1832

I awoke to the sound of birds chirping and the sun high overhead. My warm blanket made me want to stay there longer. I turned my head to see my sister, but she wasn't there. *She must be looking for something for us to eat.* I drifted off again.

When I finally awoke, the sun had grown hotter. I still didn't see my sister. For a minute longer, I lay there waiting for her to talk to me. Nothing, only a slight breeze swayed the tall bushes back and forth.

Anamosa had wrapped me very tight in my blanket, just as Mother did. I brought my arm up and firmly took hold of the blanket edge to throw it off me. I sat up and listened. Nothing, only the sounds of the birds and the rustling of leaves as the wind blew through the trees. The air held the fresh scent of rain; the grass was dry.

I knew my sister had to be close by; she wouldn't leave me alone for long. She said she would take care of me. Slowly I stood, picked up my blanket and tied it around my shoulders. I walked for a long time following the path my sister and I had taken through the tall prairie grass, picking at bushes, looking for berries. I kept turning around thinking I heard someone behind me. With each step, I wondered if I was going in the right direction. The tall cottonwoods bent with the breeze, making them all look the same. The sun shone bright directly above me when I spotted the river. Surely, we hadn't walked this far the day before. Where could my sister be?

I was thirsty. The sun began dropping behind the trees. Everything was quiet except for the lapping of water along the shore. At the river's edge, I bent down to drink. With cupped hands, I scooped up a handful of water and brought it to my mouth. *Wait. What's that? Did I hear something? Is it Anamosa?* I looked to the right when I heard the rustle of brush and saw a silhouette of an Indian brave coming toward me. From the shadows, I could see he wore a white man's shirt, breechclouts, leggings, and moccasins, but his hair was long and as black as the hair on Father's dog.

I didn't recognize him. *Is he from one of the clans that came to my village?* I turned and ran as fast as I could. My legs ran as swift as the antelope, but he was swifter. I went faster and faster, but he stayed right behind me. I didn't see the drop off and fell end over end, landing on top of my blanket. When I looked up, he stood next to me.

He spoke in a soft voice. "Don't be afraid."

He was not of my people, but I understood him. "Who are you?"

"We must get away from the river's edge before the white man comes back."

He wore white man's clothes but looked like an Indian. He wore his hair like our braves. *Maybe he'll take me to my people and find my sister?*

"I am called Askuwheteau. Come, we go together."

Askuwheteau reached for my hand and pulled me up,

then wrapped my blanket around me. He looked as old as my big brother, Kenwikomata. The look in his eyes told me he wouldn't hurt me. I took his rough, strong hand and fell in step beside him.

We followed the river, but kept our distance from the edge. At one point Askuwheteau dug up a few roots. We brushed the dirt away and ate them raw. I didn't know what kind of root it was, but Askuwheteau said it was good to eat. My stomach hurt so much. Mother had said not to think of food when you are hungry because it makes you want food even more. I think my mother spoke the truth.

Darkness fell upon us quickly. Askuwheteau found a large tree with many branches to cover us, and we took refuge next to the broad trunk. I sat next to him as he put my blanket over us to keep the dampness from settling upon us. His arms encircled me, and he drew me closer to him for warmth. My eyes were heavy from walking all day, and my stomach growled. In the distance, I heard an owl and felt comforted. My head fell against his chest, and I closed my eyes while a gentle wind blew against my face.

With my eyes tightly closed, I saw Father coming to me. "Father," I cried out, but he didn't speak. He came closer and closer until I could see his face clearly. It was covered with blood mixed with his war paint, and his eyes looked through me. He didn't know I was there. "Father, it's me, Memekeha. Why don't you speak to me?"

With outstretched arms, I waited for him to pick me up, but he walked past me. My father, a great warrior, always picked me up when he saw me. I didn't understand. I cried but he kept walking. I cried until my body shook. I felt strong arms hold me tight and someone rocked me back and forth. My eyes opened and saw only blackness.

Askuwheteau stroked my hair and softly sang. "Sleep, sleep, little one. Dream good dreams, and they will carry you far into the night. Sleep, sleep, little one." I drifted off again.

Chapter 6

August 4, 1832

The next morning I awoke alone again. I sat up straight and pulled my blanket up to my chin. *Where did Askuwheteau go? Did I do something to make him angry?* My eyes felt heavy so I rolled over and fell asleep again.

This time the dream came to me quickly. Mother ran toward me carrying Sionoh, my little brother. He was crying, and she tried to keep him quiet. "Mother, Mother, here I am," I cried out.

She didn't answer but ran past me until I couldn't see her anymore. My shoulders dropped. I turned to see my older sister, Sokanon, running toward me, her arms outstretched. I felt excited with the thought of her picking me up as she always did to make me laugh. She also ran past me, her blank eyes never saw me. Again, my shoulders slumped; I fell to the ground and cried. I missed Mother and my family and wanted to be with them, but I didn't know where they were. Anamosa was nowhere in sight either. *Am I the only one left?*

Askuwheteau touched my arm arousing me awake. "I'm sorry little one for your bad dreams. We need to keep moving to find our people."

He stooped down and gathered my blanket and me in his arms, and began walking toward the river. Leaning my head on his shoulder, the warm touch of the sun made me almost forget my rumbling stomach. Surely, Askuwheteau could hear the noise too. I stole a glance at his face. He looked like my older brother, a boy still, not quite a man. His face was long, not yet lined from age. A high forehead with dark black eyes that did not smile, maybe from the things he had seen in his young years. *Would my eyes be like that too?*

He stopped by the river and set me on the ground beside a young tree. Askuwheteau pulled at the tender bark and handed me a small piece he'd peeled from the tree. "Eat this; it will help with the hunger."

I held the bark to my mouth and took a small bite. It tore easily between my teeth. My tongue rolled it over and over while I chewed and chewed. Slowly I swallowed it and proceeded to take another bite. We sat there together, until we had eaten the rest of the bark he had broken off. At least my stomach stopped making noise, but I needed water.

"Little one, what do they call you?"

"I'm called Memekeha."

"Memekeha…" He rubbed his chin then touched the end of my nose with his finger. "I like that name. Do you have brothers or sisters?" Before I could answer, he continued. "I had two small sisters when the soldiers came into our camp. I watched as the soldiers shot them. I couldn't move." He hung his head. "I ran toward them, but was knocked down by one of the horses. I don't remember anything after that." His voice softened even more. "When I awoke, the camp was quiet."

I picked up a small stick lying at my feet and began

pushing at the leaves. As I began to speak, I looked up, and saw tears slide down his face. "I have three sisters and four brothers."

Askuwheteau laid his hand over mine. "I'm sorry about your family; we'll have to keep going if we're going to find both of our families. Maybe they will be all together when we find them."

I wanted to believe him, but it seemed like it had been days since we'd seen any of our people. *Maybe they are all dead.*

I thought Askuwheteau must be from the village my father visited sometimes. It was a two-day walk from our camp; on his return, he'd tell us stories of their braves. Father said they had strong men, then turned to my mother and with a wink said how pretty the women were, too. Mother picked up a stick and playfully hit Father's arm. Later that night in our lodge, I saw Father and Mother hold hands and snuggle together in their blankets. I could hear them softly whispering to each other.

Askuwheteau stood up and stretched. He bent down, picked me up in his arms. "If we stay close to the brush, the white man can't see us." He walked as quiet as the fox stalking his prey. Askuwheteau pushed forward into the thick brush. He finally set me on the ground and told me to walk behind him while he tried to cut a path. A branch hit my chest and some beads tore off my dress. Too tired to care, I pressed forward trying to keep up. The afternoon grew colder, so I wrapped my blanket closer around my shoulders.

We pushed deeper and deeper, until the thick brush wouldn't let us go any farther. Exhaustion overtook us both, and we fell to the ground.

"I'm hungry." Askuwheteau had heard these words before but the pain in my stomach was more than I could stand.

"Little one, I know you're hungry, but it's getting dark. If we rest here until morning, maybe we'll find something for you then."

I nodded. I removed my blanket from my shoulders and laid it on the ground. Askuwheteau helped me spread it out; then he took one side and laid it over me. The sounds of the night quickly lulled me to sleep.

Chapter 7

August 5, 1832

Fatigue quickly gave way to sleep; dreams filled every corner of my mind. I felt myself falling. Not falling fast, but floating, swirling, drifting closer to the ground. Then, as a leaf in the wind, carried me higher; I could no longer touch the ground. As I floated higher the trees below faded from my sight, and I almost touched the clouds. I felt helpless as the wind blew me about. A great eagle flew by me, his magnificent wings spread as he searched for food. Suddenly, the wind stopped. I felt myself spiral to the ground, closer and closer the land came.

I awoke with a start, my blanket over my head. I rubbed my eyes, and then opened them again. Before me lay a mound of dirt; the musty smell filled my senses. I tried to remember the last time I smelled that same odor; I finally remembered and sat up throwing my blanket to the side.

"You were having dreams again; maybe the Great Spirit spoke to you." Askuwheteau smiled at me. "I didn't want to wake you."

I stood up and grabbed my blanket. I stretched and tried to shake the dream from my mind. I didn't know what my dream meant; I didn't want to know. My mouth felt dry.

Askuwheteau rose gracefully, like a cat getting ready to pounce, he brushed leaves from his clothes. "We'll find the river and follow it. Maybe I can catch some fish today."

I rubbed my stomach and smiled. "Do you think we can? I'd like that very much."

He led the way again. It seemed like we walked a couple of miles before I heard the rippling sounds of water. Askuwheteau crouched down and motioned for me to follow. "Be quiet Me-me-ke-ha. We don't know who may be on the water."

I bent down hoping no one saw me and crept behind him. We made our way through the tall grass closer to the river. My own thoughts of family took me away, and I didn't watch where I was going.

Before I knew it, I stood at the edge of a bluff overlooking the river. Heavy timber lined the riverbanks both below me and to both sides. Askuwheteau jerked my arm, and I fell next to him on a large rock. He put his finger to his lips and pointed to a row of canoes along the water's edge across the river. From behind the trees, we saw smoke billowing into the air. We heard voices. I tried to swallow the lump in my throat. *What if they are the Ioway tribe, or the Sioux, or…*

"Wait here. Don't move or make a sound," he whispered.

I watched as he crawled over to a cluster of trees lining the ledge and disappeared, not knowing if he would come back. Everyone seemed to leave me; I didn't know what to do. I reminded myself to be quiet like Askuwheteau said.

Shaded by tall blades of grass and trees, I spread my blanket on the ground and lay down. I stared at the large white clouds rolling across the light blue sky. The feel of the gentle breeze made me sleepy. The large trees gently swayed in the breeze. One big puffy cloud looked like the great buffalo, while another looked like Father's dog running after a stick. I thought I heard voices, but they soon faded. The warmth of the sun heated my body, and I must have fallen asleep. Askuwheteau tugged on my arm and I awoke.

Without speaking, he crouched down and took my hand. I rose into a crouching position as he pulled me along behind him. Askuwheteau lowered himself over the ledge and motioned for me to follow. He put his foot on a rock then his other foot on another rock. Inch by inch he went down. I followed his every move. When we reached the bottom, we slid on our stomachs until we came to the river's edge; I saw a small raft on our side of the river I hadn't noticed before. We crawled down to the raft together. I retied my blanket around my shoulders and laid down on the raft while Askuwheteau quietly pushed it out into the water. He slowly slid into the water and pushed the raft out into the current. I lay as still as I could. Askuwheteau guided the raft to the other side of the river, right behind a line of canoes.

When we reached one of the canoes, he grabbed hold of it. He motioned for me to slide into it. I lay on the bottom but peeked over the top to watch him push all the canoes out into the water. He then came back to me and slid into the canoe with me after pushing it out into the water. We drifted into the current along with all the other canoes floating well in front of us. When we were far enough away, he started paddling. I watched as the other canoes bobbed up and down floating down the river in front, like ghost ships without anyone at the helm, sailing into the unknown.

All of a sudden, we heard war whoops and splashing

of water behind us. I turned my head toward the braves' shouts, as did Askuwheteau. We saw them fling their arms in the air. I ducked down into the canoe just as I felt the breeze from an arrow fly over my head.

My eyes fixed on Askuwheteau as he, too, lay flat inside the canoe. I watched the arrows soar high into the air, gliding, searching for their mark, then fall short into the river.

I could still hear shouting and splashing of water behind us. If they were going to follow us, they would have to find their canoes, or maybe they would run along the shore, or even try swimming to overtake us. Soon, though, we felt like we could relax as the canoe drifted down the fast-flowing river.

We moved gracefully, but swiftly over small waves, down river, while I lay on the canoe's bottom looking up into the bright sunlight. Big billowy clouds formed as I watched an eagle soar high overhead looking for his prey. *Could we be the prey of those other tribes? Were my people still fighting the white man?* I looked up into Askuwheteau's face. His eyes darted back and forth along the sides of the river searching for any movement. The soft small lines around his mouth meant he had once smiled or laughed a lot. His prominent, hooked nose seemed out of place with the rest of his face. I watched his strong arms hold the paddle as he made small swift strokes through the water. He was a great warrior like my brother.

Askuwheteau pointed ahead of the canoe and whispered, "That looks like one of the white man's keel boats."

I peered over the edge of the canoe and saw a long narrow boat with men holding long poles. At least ten men on both sides used the long poles to propel their boat. Each man walked from the front of the boat to the back with the poles in the water. Some of the men sang, but I didn't understand the words. They were approaching our canoe.

I put my hand to my mouth to keep from laughing at the funny paddles they used. They must have been paddles, because they moved the boat farther upstream. In the middle of the boat were stacks of bundles tied together. I sat up to see better, but Askuwheteau grabbed my arm and pulled me back down. "You must not be seen or heard. We cannot trust the white man, especially since they came into our camps and killed our families."

Our canoe hit shore just before the keelboat reached us. We jumped out and pulled it as far into the brush as we could, then we gathered brush to cover it so no one would see it. Askuwheteau and I lay in the bushes and watched as the boat rolled past us. One man laughed at another man and slapped him on the shoulder.

I started to stand, but Askuwheteau was quick. He grabbed my arm before I could get to my feet and pulled me back into the brush. Shaking his head, he pointed to the river. "You're too curious, Memekeha."

We lay in the brush until we could no longer hear the men singing. Askuwheteau stood and stretched. I followed his lead. My dress, once beautiful, now looked like strips of cloth hanging on tree limbs, or like deer meat drying on poles. I pulled my blanket tighter around my shoulders and reached for my pouch hanging around my neck. I rubbed my fingers across it and felt the small comb I had picked up at our lodge before Anamosa pulled me away. *Anamosa. My family. Are they all lost to me?*

Chapter 8

August 5, 1832

We reached our canoe and began pulling the brush away from it. Askuwheteau motioned for me to get in while he pushed it out into the water before climbing in himself. Dark shadows lined the riverbanks as the sun set. How long before we eat again? My thought of food never left me. Mother always had something on our campfire if we desired to fill our mouths. I could almost taste the sweet rabbit roasting on the spit above the fire, and the thought of the luscious red berries as they lingered in my mouth. The other children and I loved pulling the big juicy berries off the bushes and popping them in our mouths letting the juice slide down our chins. I rubbed my stomach. It had stopped hurting; it didn't even make noise any more.

The bottom of the canoe felt cool as I lay in it. I pulled my blanket tighter around me. From the faint light of the moon, I could barely see Askuwheteau's face. He looked tired, or maybe it was something else. I didn't understand his expression at the time, but it was the look of sadness, maybe pain. He, too, missed his mother and father as I missed mine. *Is it the thought of his two sisters that hold the look of ache in his eyes?*

My hand slipped from my blanket and fell to my side. It felt wet. I looked down, and the bottom of the canoe was filling with water. I sat up with a start. "Look, there's water in the canoe!"

Askuwheteau turned to look behind him. "There must be a leak."

He began paddling closer to shore and ran the canoe into a cove. Askuwheteau jumped out and pulled the canoe into the brush, then fell to the ground. I continued to sit in the canoe waiting for him to get up, but he didn't. I grabbed the side of the canoe and threw myself over almost losing my balance. I ran to him and dropped to my knees. He didn't move: I thought he was dead. "Are you all right?"

He didn't answer. I shook his shoulder and whispered, "Askuwheteau."

Still there was no answer or movement. I continued to shake him, but he didn't move. Brushing the dirt from his cheek and forehead, I cradled his head in my lap.

"Memekeha," Askuwheteau whispered, barely moving his lips. I pressed my ear closer to his mouth to hear him. His hand slowly came up to my face and fell back to his side.

Tears welled in my eyes, and I felt a big knot in my throat. "Please don't die," I cried. I laid my head on his chest to hear his heart beat. *He can't leave me now. Our people have to be close by.* I heard a faint beat in his chest, or was it my imagination? *He has to be alive. Maybe he's just tired. He has to be hungry like I am.* We were both tired. Tears started to flow, more tears, and I couldn't stop them. Exhausted, I wanted to be close to him, so I laid my head on Askuwheteau's chest and again fell into a restless sleep. This night the dreams did not visit me.

I felt like I'd been asleep for hours. However, when I opened my eyes and gazed along the outline of the trees, all I saw was blackness until I looked up into the sky. The stars shined so bright that night. They looked like they were twinkling, blinking off and on. *Are they trying to say something? Maybe the Great Spirit is trying to tell me something.*

My neck felt stiff, I could hardly move it. I sat up, rubbed my neck, and looked at Askuwheteau still lying at my side, so still. It took a moment for me to remember what had happened the night before. He breathed more evenly as I watched the rise and fall of his chest. I must have watched him breathe for a long time, before I finally fell asleep again.

Chapter 9

August 6, 1832

I opened my eyes and gazed at the clear blue sky. It was quiet, neither a bird singing, nor the rustle of the trees. The sun peeked over the tops of the trees. I rubbed my blurred eyes and tried to remember where I was. My mind drifted over the past few days—mother, running, water, hunger, and sleep— my arm fell to the ground hitting something warm and soft. I pushed up on one arm to get a better look. It was a moment before I realized where I was and what had happened. His shallow breathing scared me.

"Askuwheteau? Askuwheteau?" I shoved his lifeless form a few times.

"Mmmmmm."

"Askuwheteau, can you sit up?"

"Mmmmmm."

I lifted his head and tried to get him to sit up. "We must get up and try to find food. We have to keep going. Can you sit up?"

He rolled his head toward me and slightly opened his eyes. "I'm sorry, Memekeha. I'll take care of you. Let me rest for just a while longer."

I laid his head back down and pulled my blanket over

him. "I'll let you rest. I'll look for something to eat for both of us." It was my turn to take care of him.

His eyes closed before I stood up. I looked around but couldn't tell where we were. We'd been traveling for at least three days, or was it four? I couldn't tell which direction my village was now. All I knew was that the river was close. Our village was next to a river once, but we left when Black Hawk said we must leave. *How far did we go? Which direction did we go? Where did my sister take me when we had to flee our village?* My head hurt with so many questions. Questions I couldn't answer. Too tired and hungry to look for food, I sat down in a pile of damp grass. The wet grass seeped through my ragged dress to my skin, but I didn't care. Tears eased their way down my face. I wanted my mother, my father; I wanted my family. *Where are they? Why aren't they looking for me?*

With my feet stretched out before me, I looked at my moccasins. *That's funny, where are all the beads across the top of my moccasins?* My finger traced along the top of my foot where the bright red, blue, and yellow beads used to be, the beads my mother so lovingly sewed along the top. Both moccasins were missing beads. *Mother will be so angry at me when she sees them.* I pulled my legs up, hugged them with my arms, and gently swayed back and forth. With my head on my knees, and my eyes closed, I silently murmured the song my father sang to me when I didn't feel well. I wished I could find him. He would know what to do. I could tell him how Askuwheteau had taken care of me and that now he needed care.

"Hay-a-hay-a, oh Great Spirit. Hay-a-hay-a show me the way. My family looks for me, Great Leader. Give me eyes to see. Hay-a-hay-a."

I lifted my head. I heard something, something different. Looking to my right, then to my left, the sound stopped. I laid my head back down on my knees and closed my eyes again. "Hay- a- hay-a, oh Great Spirit. It has been so long. My family looks for me. Where oh where have they gone? Hay-a-hay-a..."

There's that sound again only louder. I lifted my head and looked to my left, then to my right. I looked to the top of the trees and watched as the wind blew the branches back and forth with fury. The sky darkened with eerie red streaks of clouds. Then I heard a faint rumble. It got closer and closer and the wind picked up speed. Askuwheteau lay in the open. I needed to find shelter for him. *How can I move him?*

I ran to him. "Askuwheteau, we need to find shelter." I shook him. "Can you get up?"

He turned his head to look at me, and then his gaze went skyward. "You're right; we need to find shelter. It looks like there'll be a great storm. Help me get over to the rocks."

I put his arm over my shoulder as he rolled over and got on his knees. He pushed himself up, and then fell back down on his knees again. The thunder increased and lightning streaked across the sky. He pushed up again, half dragged himself, and half walked, while I tried to help him get out of the open field. I led him to a stone ledge where he sat down, leaning against the rock. I ran back to gather my blanket just as a loud clap of thunder exploded. I jumped. For a minute, I felt as if I were back in our camp with the soldiers firing their guns. Another sharp crack of thunder and a bright streak of lightning shot across the sky. Rain fell in big drops, flattening the grass where I had been sitting.

"Thank you, Memekeha. You got us to safety just in time."

"You're welcome." I pushed his wet hair out of his eyes. "Do you feel better?"

He ran his hand across his face. "As soon as the storm stops, we can start out again. I feel rested. I must get you to your people."

I covered his hand with mine and tried to reassure him. "We'll find them soon."

It seemed like hours before the storm let up. Cold rain chilled me, and I tried to keep warm by sitting next to Askuwheteau and sharing my blanket with him. I laid my head on his arm and watched as the rain dripped off the side of the ledge. Drip. Drip. Drip. Each drop spiraled its way to the ground descending into small pools of water. *Is it raining where my mother and father are?*

"Memekeha, it's late. We should stay here in this shelter for the night. We can start out again tomorrow and maybe tomorrow will be the day we find our people."

I hung my head as I listened to him. I knew it was better to stay under cover of the ledge for the night, but I wanted to find my family. "All right, Askuwheteau. Maybe tomorrow will be a better day. Maybe it won't rain again." I lay down beside him.

He rubbed my back and tried to soothe me, but I was beginning to feel like we would never find anyone from our camp. I wondered if he felt that way, too. I no longer felt hungry, only tired. Tired of being hungry, tired of walking, tired of watching for white men, just plain tired. My mother's words whirled around in my head telling me not to whine, that Indians do not moan about things. We are proud people rising above whatever comes our way.

"Do you think we will find our people soon?" I asked.

"I'm not sure, little one. It's been many days since we've seen anyone from our clans. When we find them, we'll have big feasts telling each other what we've done since the great fighting that sent us in many directions."

"Do you think there will be dancing again, dancing all night until we can't dance any longer?"

Askuwheteau chuckled and ruffled my hair. "I'm sure of it. Now close your eyes and go to sleep. It's going to be a long day for us. Sleep, little one, sleep. Sleep in the land of dreams. Good dreams, wonderful dreams. Your future is waiting for you there."

I snuggled closer to Askuwheteau, and he put his arm around me. I was tired of wandering, searching for our people. The warmth of his body, along with my blanket, made me feel better. I soon fell asleep.

Chapter 10

August 7, 1832

The clean smell of fresh air after a summer rain filled my nostrils. The beaming sun peered through the tree branches. *We will find my mother and father today; I just know it. I feel it, and besides, Askuwheteau says so.* Eager to get going, I jumped up grabbing my blanket from around my shoulders and stretched. My blanket whipped across Askuwheteau's shoulders.

"You're in good spirits this morning, little one. Are you ready to get going?"

"Yes, I am. I'm ready to find my family today. Let's go."

When I stood up, Askuwheteau looked at me, really looked at me and shook his head. "Me-me-ke-ha, you have very little of your dress left. Let me put my shirt on you to keep you warm."

I looked down at the shreds that were left of my dress. No longer were there beads along my neck. "But what will you wear?"

"I do not need my shirt." He pulled it over his head. "Here, put your arms in the holes."

I looked down at myself and giggled as I pressed out the folds in the cloth. "This shirt is so long. I will trip."

"But you will have clothing for yourself. When we find your mother, she will make you another dress with beautiful beads, beads to match your sparkling eyes."

His words were soothing. Words I'm sure he thought I wanted to hear. Looking to the future with our families again seemed so far away.

We set out following the great river, keeping far away from the shore but close enough to see if anyone was on the river. With my blanket wrapped around my shoulders, warming me all over, we walked until the sun was high overhead. I kept my eyes downward watching where I stepped. I lost my moccasins somewhere in the mud soon after we'd started down river. After stepping on several sharp rocks, I didn't want to do that again. My sore feet bled at one time. I stopped counting the days since the fighting in our camp. It seemed like it was so long ago, but Askuwheteau said last night it had only been a few days since he found me.

I watched Askuwheteau as he pushed bushes out of our path, careful not to break branches in case someone followed us. He had large arms like my big brother. I saw places on his back that looked like scratches. Some were deep and others looked dirty, like maybe there had been deep cuts, but he didn't complain.

The timber got thicker as we pushed on. The afternoon sun had trouble peeking through the tall willows and each bush scratched my legs. I felt tired again. *Will I ever feel like running and playing? All I want to do is sit down.* "Can we stop? How much farther do we have to go?"

He turned back to me. "Little one, we have to push on. We can't take time to stop. We have to find food."

I knew he was right, but I was hungry and tired. "Just

leave me here. You go on."

"No, little one. We've come this far together. I'll get you food." His large hand encased mine as he gently pulled me behind him. "Come."

Askuwheteau stopped suddenly. He put his finger to his lips as he turned to me. I stood still and listened. We both heard it at the same time. Dogs barking. Then we heard a man's voice. We both fell to the ground and started crawling forward. The voice got louder, but it sounded tender. The man talked to the dogs. His soothing voice calmed the dogs; they stopped barking. *Dare I try to look up to see?*

Chapter 11

August 7, 1832

We quietly crawled to the edge of the willows and brush. There we saw a large clearing of land with trees and rows and rows of fall grapes. Lots of grapes. My mouth watered at the thought of eating them. My stomach lurched. Being quiet now was the last thing on my mind as I jumped up and ran toward the first vine. I shoved the ripe grapes in my mouth and let the sweet, red juice drip down my chin. From the corner of my eye, I saw Askuwheteau run past me. He grabbed a handful, too. Two of the large dogs ran toward us. Eeeiiiikkkkkk.

Askuwheteau rushed toward the nearest tree and made a big leap like a squirrel to the first branch. He sat on the branch as the dogs jumped all around the bottom of the tree barking.

I started running toward the man who made his way to see what the dogs had cornered. All I could think of was to get away from the dogs. As soon as the man got close enough, I ran right into his arms, my hands full of the grapes. "Kookush. Quasheean."

I don't know why I said that, but all I could think of was food. Pemmican and bread, was my favorite. My mother made the best flat bread, and the thought of hot bread made my mouth water.

He held me tight and said something to the dogs. They backed away from the tree and lay down. The man started laughing. "Kookush."

Did he understand me?

"Yes, yes, there now." He patted my back. "Pigmeat and bread, but where did you come from?" He looked behind me to see if there might be someone else.

His Indian tongue was different, but I understood him. I wondered how he knew my language. I turned my head toward the river and pointed. "We came from the great river."

He turned around to Askuwheteau and motioned for him to come down from the tree. "The dogs won't hurt you." He motioned to a boy running toward us. "Samuel, go help that boy down from the tree."

The man held me close as we watched Askuwheteau slowly descend the tree. He winced once he reached the bottom and sat down at the trunk of the tree. His head bobbed forward; and then he didn't move. Still holding me, the man ran to his side saying something I didn't understand. He sat me on the ground as he kneeled down beside Askuwheteau.

He yelled in his strange language. The big man bent down to see what was wrong with Askuwheteau.

I turned to see a woman in a pretty dress coming from a small lodge with several children trailing behind her. This man had many children. I thought he must be an important man; maybe he was a chief. His lodge looked like the buildings I saw at the fort when my father took me with him one time.

The dogs continued to bark and ran around while the children giggled and stared at us. One girl came up to me and touched my hair. Her warm smile made me feel at ease. Her golden hair was pulled back from her face with a thin piece of colorful cloth.

She reached for my hand. I pulled back. She reached for my hand again. I studied her face. I looked down at her hand and back into her eyes. Slowly I took her hand and followed her to the lodge glancing to my left and right. I don't know what I thought I'd see but still fearful of someone jumping out at me. We walked behind the man who carried Askuwheteau and the woman who held the hand of the younger girls.

The woman's long dress moved from side to side as she walked. It made a swishing sound as it moved back and forth. I'd never seen a dress like that before. Small black and white squares covered it. She wore a big white dress over her skirt held up by strings that tied in the back. Her long brown hair twisted into a knot on top of her head. I wondered why she didn't wear beads on her dress as my mother did.

As soon as we got to the door of their lodge, the woman turned to me and pointed to the side of the building. She said something I didn't understand, but I followed the little girl who had been holding her hand, and sat down next to her. We all leaned against the lodge. The man carried Askuwheteau inside.

I listened to the sounds coming from the lodge so intently that I didn't notice the young girl tugging on my hair. I turned to face her and she smiled at me. She tried to run her fingers through my hair, but it was tangled. She kept pulling my hair, making my head jerk. I put my hand up to my head and gave her a look that should have stopped the meanest cat around, but she smiled again, and kept trying to detangle my hair with her fingers. I grabbed her hand and put it down to her side. When I did this, my pouch fell loose from my neck. I picked it up and held it close to my chest.

The two girls sat on each side of me. One looked to be a few years older than I was, and the smaller one was probably my age. The older boy went inside with the big man and the woman. One boy sat outside across from the girls and me. They talked between themselves. I wished I could understand them. They seemed friendly.

I felt the familiar object in my pouch. My fingers played with the string as I wondered if I should open it or not. Then the girl started running her fingers through my hair again jerking my head back. "Atwe! Ouch!"

I untied the pouch and pulled out my mother's comb. Her beautiful comb Father carved out of buffalo bone. Both girls' eyes lit up. The smaller girl stood up and moved closer to get a better look. I held it close to me. She looked at the comb then back at me. "You can touch it." They looked at each other then back to me. The older one frowned. I gingerly held the comb out for them to touch.

Both girls sat back down beside me as the little girl's finger traced the carvings that lined the rim. I held the comb up and said, "My father made this for my mother."

She looked at me, then back at the comb, I realized then she didn't know my language. Suddenly she jumped up, grabbed my comb, and ran inside the lodge. I abruptly stood up. That was my comb. A minute later the big man stepped through the door; I knew he had to be her father. The girl stood beside him and handed him my comb. She said something. He took my comb and looked at me. "Is this yours?"

Relief, the man who spoke my language. "Yes, my father made it for my mother."

He turned to the girl and said something. This was strange talk to me. I wished I could understand. She smiled as she walked toward me and sat down by me.

"My name is Mr. Jordan." The big man said. "What is your name? What is the name of your brother?"

"My name is Memekeha, but that is not my brother. His name is Askuwheteau."

Mr. Jordan sat down next to me and his children gathered around him. "He'll be fine. Did you know Askuwheteau was shot eleven times? I don't know how he made it as far as he did with you. If he's not your brother, do you know what village he's from?"

He said something to his children, but the only thing I understood was my name.

Shot eleven times. So that was why he had those marks all over his back. He's very brave. "No, I don't know his village, but I think it maybe the village my father visited often. It was close to ours. Askuwheteau is not of my clan. I am Sauk, and I think he is Fox."

"Well, well, well, that makes sense. It appears he's taken very good care of you. We'll let him rest for now, at least until he regains his strength."

The younger boy stood beside Mr. Jordan and eyed me with suspicion. Mr. Jordan rubbed the boy's hand. "This is my son Samuel, and the other boy is Andrew. I have two other sons, Thomas and Benjamin who are married and live quite a distance from us." He motioned to the older girl. "This is Amanda and Elsie is sitting next to you. My two other girls, Phoebe and Diana, live in Iowa, also quite a distance from here. And I can't forget Bear; behind you is Bear, our dog.

As he motioned to each child, I looked at them and wondered what they were thinking of me. *I must look a sight.* My hair was no longer in the beautiful braids Mother made, and my clothing was in shreds. I wore a white man's shirt, and no longer had moccasins on my feet. And I was still hungry. My stomach made a loud growl.

Mr. Jordan laughed. He said something to Samuel.

I shook his arm to get his attention. "Kat-e-quah. Kat-e-quah. My mother's name, Kat-e-quah. I think it means eagle because she sees very good. Do you know where my mother is?" The tears began to slide down my cheek. "My name is Memekeha." I brushed at my eyes with the back of my hand. I would not let these people see me cry.

"No, my child, I don't know where your mother could be. You say her name is Kat-e-quah?" With his large rough but kind hands, he pushed my hair back away from my face and looked at his woman standing behind me. "But we must give you a name while you are with us. A name that is easier for everyone to say. Is it all right, if we call you Katie? It sounds a lot like your mother's name. I think that's the perfect name for you. Besides, when I think of the name Katie, I don't think of an eagle, I think of a butterfly. You look like a little butterfly—fragile, and yet strong."

I could not control the tears any longer and buried my head in my hands. "My father gave me the name of Memekeha. It means butterfly. Will I ever see him again?"

The big man put his arms around my shoulder and patted me on the back. "Now, now Katie, it's going to be all right, but I don't know if you will see your father again.

We'll do what we can to find him for you. For now, you can call me Father Jordan and my wife Mother Jordan if that would make you feel better."

I looked into his kind face and felt at peace. Drying my eyes with the back of my hand, I looked at Mother Jordan as she stroked the top of the girl's head he called Amanda. Amanda smiled at me. This family would take Askuwheteau and me into their lodge and show us kindness. I did not feel afraid, but I wished I could understand what they were saying.

One of the boys came out of their lodge with something in his hand. He rubbed his stomach and handed it to me.

I looked at Father Jordan. He smiled. "Go ahead, Katie, eat. You'll feel better with something in your stomach. It's Mother Jordan's cornbread." Again, he said something to Samuel who ran back into the lodge.

I sat down by Father Jordan and started eating the cornbread. It felt thick and coarse on my tongue; pieces of it started to crumble in my hand. I quickly licked the crumbs from my hands and ate some more. It tasted sweet and gritty, unlike anything I'd tasted before. The boy Father Jordan called Samuel returned with a cup of milk and handed it to me. I grabbed it and took a big drink. It was cool and creamy as I let it slide down my throat, washing the bread down to my stomach with a slosh. Rubbing my stomach, I felt full for the first time since fleeing our camp with my sister. I watched Mother Jordan and Amanda go back and forth to the lodge. Then in a few more minutes, Mother Jordan stepped into the doorway and called out to Father Jordan.

Samuel jumped up and ran toward the door where a table sat with a big bowl on top and a large piece of cloth beside the bowl. Father Jordan reached down for my hand, pulled me up and pushed me toward the lodge. I stood in line behind the little girl, Elsie. They all walked up to the bowl and washed their hands, and then dried them on the cloth. Before Elsie walked away, she turned and handed me a small brown bar that felt rough. Then she took my hands with the bar and put them in the bowl of water swishing them around. I followed her actions and wiped my hands on the cloth, too.

After washing, each child went into the lodge and sat down on a bench at a table. Mother Jordan motioned for me to sit between her and Father Jordan. I squeezed in between them not knowing what else to do. No one ate anything. Everyone sat quietly with their hands on their laps. My family sat on the ground with our food in our hands. We do not wait. Father Jordan spoke softly. I didn't understand what he said, so I watched everyone. Everyone bowed their heads and closed their eyes. When Father Jordan stopped talking, each head came up and they started to eat. *Strange ritual.*

After their meal, Father Jordan let me go into their sleeping room to check on Askuwheteau. He was still asleep. I stood watching the rise and fall of his chest just as I had in the past. I laid my hand on his chest and whispered, "Heya- heya- heya- heya. Oh, Great Spirit, make him well. Make him swift as the deer again. Heya- heya- heya- heya."

. . .

I heard muffled noises coming from outside. I went to the door of the cabin and saw Father Jordan sitting next to a small fire. He motioned for me to join Amanda on her blanket. When I reached her, she stared at me as she moved her leg over leaving no room for me to sit. I stood there looking at each one's faces, wondering what I should do. Father Jordan said something in a stern voice to Amanda. She lowered her gaze then slowly moved her leg back leaving room for me. Father Jordan smiled and motioned for me to sit down. Mother Jordan sat across from me, next to the youngest girl.

Father Jordan sat next to me. "Katie, when the weather is good, we come outside at night and have family time. We talk about what we've done during the day and praise God for the day He gave us. We would like you to join us." He bowed his head. "Heavenly Father, thank you for this day. Be with us through the night. Amen." He said this in both my language and his.

I lowered my head like the others, but then slowly opened my eyes, looking up to watch each person. I wondered who he was talking to. Each head was bowed and their eyes were closed, just like when they sat down to eat. When Father Jordan finished speaking, everyone said one word. I wished I knew what they were saying. Then everyone stood up and gathered their blankets. Amanda took the end of hers and pulled it, making me roll off into the dirt. I wasn't sure, but I was beginning to feel like she didn't like me.

Father Jordan turned and walked toward their lodge with Mother Jordan right behind him. Each child, with blanket in hand, followed. One by one, they entered their lodge. I sat there in the dirt wondering where I should go and then spotted my blanket by the lodge door. I ran over and picked it up.

Father Jordan poked his head out the door, "Katie, aren't you coming in?"

My blanket felt comforting as I ran the fur across my lips.

It felt rough yet familiar with its warm bristles caressing my cheek and mouth. "Did you want me to come in?"

"Dear Katie, you can't sleep outside. Come in here and sleep with everyone else. There is room for you. Come along."

I followed Father Jordan into the lodge. Two corners of the sleeping room held a bed unlike anything my family slept on. The beds were made of wood and in the shape of a box. Each box had blankets with big fluffy mounds of material of many colors. Since Askuwheteau slept on Father and Mother Jordan's box they slept on Samuel and Andrew's box. Amanda and Elsie went to their box and quickly pulled the blankets back and got in, throwing the covers up to their chins. Samuel and Andrew took their blankets and laid them on the floor, then lay down, covering themselves up with another blanket. Father Jordan pointed to the bed Amanda was lying in and said, "Katie we've made a pallet on the floor beside Amanda and Elsie's bed. Tomorrow we'll find more suitable arrangements for you."

I watched as Father and Mother Jordan went to the empty bed and sat down. The floor looked more inviting than trying to sleep in a box. I took my blanket and lay down. The only thing missing was the buffalo hide I used and made soft by Mother. I wanted to feel my mother's touch right now. I wanted her to wrap me in my blanket as she did every night before the attack on our camp.

I didn't know how tired I was until I lay down.

As soon as I closed my eyes, I fell into a deep slumber. Vastness enclosed me, and I was sure I was standing, but I felt bottomless. With eyes tightly closed, I saw bright lights—reds, yellows, and orange. Out of the yellow light, a black horse came riding toward me. Upon his back

Askuwheteau, his face painted black with yellow stripes under his eyes, and a red stripe going from his forehead to the end of his nose. In his hair, he wore a lone eagle feather with beads and leather strips. The black horse charged forward. I was too scared to move. As he approached, Askuwheteau leaned down and scooped me up on his horse. He told me to hang on; he would keep me safe. I wrapped my arms around his waist and pressed my face against his back. I felt the muscles of the horse as he flew over each rise and fall of the land. We rode like the wind blowing over tall prairie grass. I felt at peace.

Chapter 12

August 8, 1832

I opened my eyes and stared into the face of one of Father Jordan's big furry dogs licking my nose. I pushed him away, pulled the blanket over my head, and burrowed down. Someone pushed me. I threw the blanket aside and sat up. The dog stood beside me wagging his tail and drooling as he tried to lick my face again. What did he want with me? "Awanewa." I pushed at him.

Amanda started laughing and said strange words to me. She stood in the doorway with her hand over her mouth as she tried to hold back her laughter. Her yellow dress looked like the same dress she wore the day before, but I hadn't noticed the blue flowers on it.

"Make him go away." *Did she understand what I said?*

She came over and sat down rubbing the dog's head. She pushed the dog away then pulled the dog back pointing to him.

I saw her lips move and heard sounds but could not understand. *Will I ever understand what they're saying? I hope I won't need to. I plan to return to my own village with my own family as soon as we find them.*

Amanda's hair, the older girl's, was gold; gold as the

buttercups that grew along the shores of the mighty river. I had never seen hair as light as hers. Long brown eyelashes encased her dark brown piercing eyes. Last night I thought she didn't want to be friends, but this morning she was talking to me. I wished I knew what she was saying. I sat cross-legged with my head in my hands.

She pulled the dog closer to me and then pointed back to the dog. "Bear. B...e...a...r."

I must have had a bewildered look on my face because she threw her hands in the air and made a face growling at me. "Bear, Katie, Bear."

Just then, Father Jordan came into the room. "Mankawa. His name is Mankawa, Bear. Like the bears your people hunt for food."

Mankawa. "Father Jordan, why do they name him Bear? Bears are scary."

He laughed. "Because he is scary to strangers who wander onto our farm, but he is a big, soft, cuddly baby to the family. He lets us know if there is an intruder, and, I can see he likes you Katie."

"I don't know." I said. "But if that's his name, then, yes. Mankawa. Bear. Bear."

Amanda clapped her hands. "B...e...a.....r?" She laughed. "That's it, Katie. Bear. Go away, Bear."

I watched as she walked away with the dog following her. She woke the younger boy by tugging on his blanket until he sat up and rubbed his eyes. She smoothed the hair of the smallest girl, Elsie, when she walked by only stopping long enough to give her a kiss on the forehead. Amanda turned back and looked at me, then just as quick headed out the door giggling.

The young boy, Samuel, looked at me and then around

the room. He wrinkled his nose and said something as he pointed to me.

The young girl, Elsie, began to laugh. I heard an "a-hem" behind me as Mother Jordan cleared her throat. Everyone got quiet. I turned to find her standing in the doorway. She wiped her hands on her white dress as she spoke sternly to Samuel. Elsie walked outside with Mother Jordan.

I didn't know what she wanted me to do so I sat still. Samuel walked by me and touched my shoulder. He motioned for me to follow him. When he reached the door, and I hadn't moved yet, he turned around and came back. He grabbed my hand and pulled me to my feet.

I followed him outside to the table with the bowl on top from the night before. It was filled with fresh water this morning. The older boy, Andrew, wiped his face while Amanda wiped Elsie's, face with the piece of cloth. Samuel gave me a shove toward the bowl. *Did he want me to splash water on my face, too?* When I didn't move, he took my hand and walked with me over to the bowl. He put his hand in the water, turned to look at me, then brought his hand to his face and splashed water all over it.

I giggled.

Samuel looked so funny with water streaming down his face. *Did they do this every morning?*

Mother Jordan came to my side, took my hands, and dipped them in the bowl, then tenderly brought the cool water to my face. The water felt refreshing as it streamed down my arms and face. I turned to see Samuel wipe his face on the cloth. Mother Jordan took both of my hands again, put them in the water and brought the cool liquid to my face. She spoke slowly to me, but I still didn't understand her words.

"Katie, Mother Jordan wants you to wash your face like the other children." I finished washing and then turned to Father Jordan.

"Father Jordan, how am I supposed to know what they're saying?"

"Katie, give it time." He motioned for me to follow everyone back into the lodge. Seated at the table again with their hands on their laps the family waited for me.

Father Jordan bowed his head. "Katie, we praise God for another day. Just maybe, Askuwheteau will be able to join us today."

"I want to see him. Is he awake?"

"Not now, Katie, I just checked on him, and he was sitting up. I'm not sure he's strong enough yet to get out of bed, at least not as strong as I thought he might be. Let us bow our heads. Katie, bow your head like the others."

I watched everyone bow their heads and close their eyes. He wanted me to do the same. I bowed my head but didn't close my eyes like the others. Why do they close their eyes? Who don't they want to see?

"Heavenly Father, thank you for giving us this day. Father, thank you for Katie and thank you for our food. Amen."

Again, he said this in my tongue and then in theirs. *I understand what he said, but who is Father? Is he talking to his father? Where is he?* I raised my head to see if someone else had joined us in the circle. I looked around at each child, then to Father Jordan and Mother Jordan, but no one else was there. This was all so strange. Would I ever understand what they were doing or saying? I wanted my own family. My own ways.

After Father Jordan said "Amen" Mother Jordan

and Amanda stood up. They both carried a big steaming pot from the fireplace to the table and began scooping something onto each plate. Amanda took the first plate to Father Jordan. This went on until each one had a plate of food before them.

I looked down at my food and wondered what it was. Before I could pick the yellow mixture up with my fingers, Bear knocked my plate to the floor with his nose and licked my plate clean.

"No, no, bad dog, Bear," yelled Amanda.

It almost looked like Bear smiled at me while he wagged his tail and licked his face. *Did he want me to feed him again?* Amanda came over and took my plate while shooing Bear away. Everyone laughed, even Father Jordan.

"I'm sorry, Katie. Bear will do that sometimes. Amanda will get you another plate of scrambled eggs," Father Jordan said.

Eggs? I did not know eggs. I wondered where they got them.

Father Jordan handed his plate to Mother Jordan. "Katie, do you know how old you are?

"I do not understand."

"Do you know how many years you are? Like Amanda is eight years old and Elsie is six. Do you know when your birthday is?"

Mother Jordan sat down beside Father Jordan and looked at me. A few minutes passed before she said anything. Mother Jordan spoke for a while, and then Father Jordan said, "You have lost a tooth already, is that not right? So Mother Jordan said you must be about seven years old. Elsie lost her first tooth at six and so did Amanda. Two of the boys lost theirs at six too. Well, we're going to say you are seven."

I still did not understand what they were talking about. *What is birthday? How many years am I?*

After the morning meal, Father Jordan stood up and motioned for me to follow him to the sleeping room. "Let's go in and check on Askuwheteau. I know you're worried about him."

Father Jordan didn't know how much I worried. Askuwheteau was my only link to my people. Without him, I felt lost. How would I find my mother and father without him? He was the only one who knew where our villages were. He was the only one who could track our steps back from where we came. My heart ached for him and for me.

I entered the small, dark room behind Father Jordan and followed him to the box where Askuwheteau lay. He was so still. His chest rose and fell with each shallow breath he took. I clutched his hand and sat down in the only chair in the room.

Father Jordan patted my head. "Katie, I'll leave you alone with Askuwheteau," he said with a soft voice. "I'll be back in a little bit to get you." Father Jordan turned and left the room, leaving me to hold Askuwheteau's hand. This room was much smaller than the other two rooms. There was only enough room for a bed and the chair I sat on.

I held his hand with both of my hands then put it next to my cheek feeling his warmth. He began to make low moaning sounds. I stood up and put my ear next to his mouth to see if I could understand what he was saying. "Memekeha, are you all right?"

"Yes, yes, I'm all right. You must get well quickly so we can go find our families. I had a dream last night that you carried me away on a big black horse. We were going to find our people. I hope you are in good health soon so we can find them. Father Jordan is taking good care of us. His woman has made meals to fill my stomach and yours."

He opened his eyes and smiled. It seemed to take all his strength to smile. "I'll be ready to take you back to your people in a couple of days. Don't give up on me. I promised I would take care of you."

I lay my head on his chest and felt a stronger beat of his heart. Much stronger than when we first arrived. "Great Spirit," I whispered, "make him well. Just get well. Then we can find our people."

That seemed to satisfy him. He closed his eyes and went back to sleep. I sat down next to him again and held his hand. My fingers traced each of his fingers then over the fingertips. I didn't know Father Jordan had entered the room until he whispered in my ear. "Come along; we don't want to tire him out. Mother Jordan has something for you."

Startled, I looked up at Father Jordan then placed Askuwheteau's hand on his chest, rose and followed Father.

He took me around the side of the lodge to where Mother Jordan, Amanda, and Elsie stood. Beside them sat a large tub. Father Jordan gave me a shove toward the tub, and he turned to leave. I turned to see where he was going and started to follow. He spun around. "No, no, dear child. Mother Jordan wants to give you a bath. You know bath. You will get in the tub, and she will pour water over you. Now go over and get in the tub. It's all right. She won't hurt you. I'll be back when you are finished."

Now why would I need to get in the tub? What is a bath? I walked slowly over to where she stood. Mother Jordan wiped her hands on her white dress and motioned for me to get into the water.

As I stepped into the tub of hot water, Mother Jordan began pulling my shirt off. I grabbed at it. She said something, but I didn't understand. Why is she taking Askuwheteau's shirt? I don't have any clothes. The more she pulled, the more I grabbed. It felt like a game of tug of war like our warriors did on game days. Then Amanda held up a pretty blue dress with small squares on it and pointed to me, then back to the dress. I let go of the shirt, looked at Mother Jordan, and slowly sat down in the tub of water as my shirt was pulled above my head.

The water felt warm on my skin. Mother Jordan picked up the brown bar we used on our hands, along with a piece of cloth, rubbed them together, and then began scrubbing on me. This was not how my mother or my sisters cleaned, but I sat there until she finished. At least I thought she was through, so I stood up and started to get out of the tub. She gently pushed me back into the water. She scooped the water into a bowl and poured it over my head. Then with the same brown bar she began rubbing it all over my hair. More water, then more bar. I sputtered. Just when I thought she was finally finished, she poured some liquid that smelled like sour grapes over my head. I wrinkled my nose. Mother Jordan chuckled. She poured a little more and motioned for me to stand. She had a big piece of cloth in her hand and wrapped me in it. *If this was what these people did all the time, I didn't want any part of it.*

After Mother Jordan completely dried me off, she began rubbing my hair with the piece of cloth. It hurt. Amanda handed me another piece of white material with strings on the top. She motioned for me to put my leg in one side and then the other leg in the other side. Then she pulled it up to my waist and tied it. She said they were bloomers.

I wished I knew what she was talking about. I looked down at my feet. The soft material against my skin felt unlike anything I'd ever worn before. Next she held her arms high so I would do the same, then she brought the dress down over my head and my arms out the sleeves. Mother Jordan stood behind me tying it at my neck.

My eyes traced each square down to the ground, and I could see my feet just below the dress. I wiggled my toes and giggled. I ran my hands over the material then looked up at Mother Jordan who smiled at me.

I wanted to learn their language so I would understand them, even if I planned to leave and find my people. I would be able to tell my father what the white man was saying. I would be able to speak for my people. Then I could tell the white man what they have done to my people by taking their land. *Yes, I will learn the white man's language.*

Mother Jordan motioned for me to follow her and the girls to a chair next to the lodge. She sat down and pulled me close to her; she tried to run her fingers through my hair. I grabbed my hair. "Eeyiiiii!"

"Katie," Mother Jordan said as she tried to push my hands down to my sides.

I turned to look for my pouch. Amanda must have been thinking the same thing, because she handed my mother's comb to me.

I grabbed it from her and handed it to Mother Jordan. With each stroke through my hair I thought of my mother. *Mother, I will find you; I know I will.*

A long low moaning sound, like a frightened child crying in the night, made me turn toward the river. Amanda, Mother Jordan, and Elsie laughed.

At that moment, Father Jordan came running from the barn. "It's all right, Katie. It's only the riverboat stopping for supplies. That's their whistle you hear. They won't stay very long. Do you want to go with me to the dock and see what they need?"

"Yes, Father Jordan. I've seen the boats on the water but never close."

"Then come along. Come on, girls, you can come too." he spoke to Mother Jordan and the girls. Father Jordan and I walked toward the sound with Father Jordan's arm on my shoulder. With his other hand, he held on to Elsie's small hand.

Chapter 13

August 8, 1832

When we approached, the boat had already pulled alongside the long wooden planks. The buzz of people talking and the sounds of lapping water against the boat, mingled with the whistle while the ropes being thrown made a whap sound when it landed on the dock. I looked at the top deck of the boat and saw some of my people holding onto the rails. I could feel myself getting excited at the thought of seeing my family. Quickly scanning each face, I searched for my mother and father. Before I could say anything, I saw one of my sisters, and then my aunt, and then another one of my sisters. Surely my mother and father were there, too, and maybe my brothers. I started to run for the boat, but Father Jordan grabbed my shoulder tight. "Wait a minute, Katie. Do you think you see someone you know?"

"Yes, Father Jordan, I see my sisters and my aunt. Let me go. I have to go." I struggled to break free of his grip.

Father Jordan tightened his grip on my arm. "Katie, you can't help them. You stay here with Amanda and Elsie. The captain is a friend of mine. Let me talk to him first. We'll see if we can't work something out."

White fists tightened and my feet planted firmly on the dock I demanded to know. "Why can't I go see my sisters?"

Father Jordan didn't answer me.

I stood watching, feeling helpless as Father Jordan walked toward the boat. Samuel and Andrew held onto the ropes the men on the boat threw toward shore. They tied the ropes to big stumps of wood along the wood planks. My sisters waved to me and cried. My heart ached as I fell to my knees; tears rolled down my cheeks. My sisters' faces were caked with dirt, and their clothing looked torn just as mine had been. I ran my hand over my skirt and felt its soft fabric.

I saw some of my mother's friends standing behind my sisters. They waved to me. If they were on the boat, then my mother must be there, too. I scanned each face again searching for my mother or my father.

I watched Father Jordan as he stood beside the boat and waited. A man wearing a white hat and coat stepped forward and shook his hand. Both men talked and laughed. Father Jordan put his hand on the shoulder of the other man and began walking toward me. Maybe he will take me to see my sisters.

Father Jordan stopped in front of me. "Katie, this man is Captain Throckmorton, and he has orders to take everyone down river to Jefferson Barracks. I know you don't understand, but it is for the best. He says he will let you go aboard to talk to your sisters for a short while. Would you like to do that?"

"Yes, I want to be with my sisters. Is my mother and father there, too?"

I watched his weathered face as he smoothed his white beard. He knelt down and looked me right in the eyes. "I'm sorry, little lady, Katie, but I don't know your parents, but please go aboard and see your sisters."

I didn't understand him and turned around to Father Jordan who then told me what he said. When I looked into Captain Throckmorton's soft brown eyes, I felt comfortable and secure. I wondered why he had to take everyone to the fort. My people didn't live in a fort like the white man. But at the time, I felt he must know what was best.

I started walking fast toward the boat. Faster, then faster, until I was running, I couldn't get to the boat quick enough. I jumped from the dock to the plank going onto the boat and jumped again when I reached the boat, then began running up the stairs to my sisters. My heart beat so fast, like it wanted to jump out of my chest.

When I reached the top of the stairs, I examined each face looking back at me. Their eyes told me what my heart didn't want to hear. *Strange how you know how a person feels without a word even being said.* I ran to the rail and found my two sisters crying. Streaks of brown dirt mixed with their tears streamed down their faces as they raced toward me. We embraced each other all at one time; we cried. Then in unison, we began asking questions.

"Where are Mother and Father?" I asked.

"How did you get here?" Ootadabun asked.

"Who is that man you came with?" Sokanon said. She wiped away the tears with the back of her hand. "The last time I saw Mother, she was running into the river with Sionoh. Everyone was trying to get to the other side."

Ootadabun said, "I was trying to get away when I tripped and fell. Before I could get up, the white man pulled me up and pushed me along into the group of others he had captured. I couldn't run fast enough. I lost sight of Father and Kenwikomata. I didn't see Mother or Sionoh."

We sat down on the floor of the boat and wept together. "We have found each other, now we will be together," Ootadabun said through tears.

Sokanon took my hands and looked into my face. "No, I don't want you to stay with us. You have to stay here. We don't know where we're going and what's going to happen to us. You are better off here."

I clung to my sister's arm. "No, I want to go, too. I want us to be together."

Ootadabun dried her tears. She ran her fingers over my dress and hair and snorted. "Look at you, dear sister. You look like the white man. You've already fit in with them. Is this not a better place for you? They'll teach you their ways. Sokanon is right. We don't know where we will go, or what our future holds." She continued running her hand down my dress and gave the bow in my hair a flip.

"Yes, yes, she's right," Sokanon chimed in. "I heard the same talk that they are taking us down river to some white man's camp and from there we don't know where we will go. You are better off here."

We clung to each other. I couldn't let them leave without me. We sat huddled together, clinging to each other's words while others moved to the side of the boat. They talked among themselves. Some pointed to something on shore. We went to the railing with the rest to see.

I saw Andrew and Samuel walking with a couple of the men from the boat leading five head of cows and carrying four big baskets full of corn. *What are they doing?* Father Jordan continued talking to Captain Throckmorton who smoked a cigar.

"What are they doing? What are they saying?" Sokanon

asked.

"I don't know."

Ootadabun grabbed my arm and twirled me around. "What do you mean you don't know? How long have you been in their camp? You should know what they are saying by now?"

"Leave her alone." Sokanon pushed her away from me and drew me to her side. "She hasn't been with them long enough to know their language. We are all upset right now."

I didn't know what to say. "I can learn their language." I wanted to please my sister. "I've only been with them a few nights."

Tears welled up in Ootadabun's eyes. "You are right little one. You're much too young to have all of this come upon you. I'm sorry." She gave me a hug. "I'll say it again; you must stay with this family. Our future does not hold much promise."

I looked over the railing. Father Jordan and Captain Throckmorton seemed to be friends, otherwise why would they smoke together? I watched with curiosity as each man laughed, then puffed on their cigars. A couple of times Father Jordan slapped Mr. Throckmorton on the shoulder and looked serious as he spoke. *Who is this man called Father Jordan? Is he important? Important enough for the captain of the boat to smoke a cigar with him? Father Jordan's lodge did not say that he had an abundance of cows or that he had much land. Or did he?*

People began crushing me against the rails to see what transpired below. Someone spoke above the din of voices. "Nenothwa." They were hungry. They wanted food. My stomach was full; theirs were empty. How could I be so unfeeling when my people were hungry? Even Askuwheteau had been given food and a clean bed. His wounds were cleaned and mended.

I turned to my sister. "When was the last time you had something to eat?"

"I don't remember." Sokanon hung her head. "I don't think about it."

"Father Jordan." I waved to Father Jordan. "Father Jordan, my sister is hungry."

Father Jordan looked up and waved. "Katie, come down here. I want to talk to you."

I glanced at my sister, then back at Father Jordan. I wanted to stay; I couldn't leave her.

Sokanon gave me a hug. "How come this man speaks our language? See, you dress like the white man already. You have forgotten our dress quickly. You even comb your hair like the white woman. Where are your moccasins? Go. Go, see what he wants of you." She gave me a shove.

I leaned down and whispered in my sister's ear, "I'll come back and bring you something to eat." Slowly I walked toward the stairs. I felt hands on my shoulders, pulling on my hair; I heard murmuring.

"Why does she leave? Why is she dressed in white man's clothes? Does she forget our ways so soon?" I wanted to run. *Why are they talking about me like this? I've done nothing wrong.*

With great speed, my feet sailed down the stairs. I was out of breath by the time I reached Father Jordan. "Please, Father Jordan, please can we give my sisters something to eat? They are so hungry."

His strong arms reached down and picked me up. Cigar smoke from his breath and clothing filtered up my nose making me sneeze. "Dear Katie, Captain Throckmorton will make sure they have food. The boys have brought some cattle and corn down to the dock for them. They'll be taken care of. The captain is a good man and will keep his word. He'll feed everyone."

I took his face in my hands and searched it for answers. "Then can I stay with them?"

Father Jordan looked at the captain then back to me. "Katie, that's not a good idea. The boat will leave in the morning and go down river. Let them have their food and a good night's rest, then in the morning, we can come back so you can say goodbye to them."

I tried to push him away. "No."

He wouldn't let go of me.

"No. I can't leave them. I have to stay with them. My mother and father will be looking for us. No. I have to stay with them."

He tightened his grip on me. The more I pulled away from him, the tighter he held me. "Katie, please listen to me. Where they have to take your sisters is not a good place. I want to make sure you are taken care of." He tried to lay my head on his shoulder, but I fought to get away from him. I had to stay with my family. They were all I had. "Katie, look at me." He took my chin in his hand so I had to look at him. "From what Captain Throckmorton has told me, it is very unlikely your parents are alive."

I beat my fists on his chest. "No. They are alive. They are." Tears rolled down my face and blurred my vision. These people did not know what they were saying. My father was an honorable and strong warrior. He had always come home from hunting, every time. My mother was a fierce fighter. She fought wild dogs to protect her family. I cried. "I know they are alive. They will be worried when they cannot find me."

"We'll go home now, little Butterfly," Father Jordan said. He held me tight as he carried me to his lodge.

I couldn't control the tears any longer as they burst forth and flowed down my cheeks. When he called me little Butterfly all I could think of was my father. My strong warrior Father.

In all the excitement of seeing my sisters, I almost forgot about Askuwheteau. When we arrived home, he was sitting outside with Mother Jordan. It looked like she was cleaning his wounds and putting a new dressing on them. She was talking to him, and I'm sure he didn't understand her any more than I did, but he watched every move she made.

He would be strong again very soon. With his good arm, he waved to me as Father Jordan carried me in the house. If I hadn't been so tired, I would have stayed and talked with him. *I must do that tomorrow.*

Every ounce of strength I had was spent crying, so when Father Jordan laid me on the box, I rolled over and buried my head in the pillow. He covered me with my blanket. My blanket; I rubbed my hand over the fur and thought of my mother. After that day, the feeling deep in the pit of my stomach led me to believe what Father Jordan said was true.

I closed my eyes and tried to see my mother…her hair pulled back from her face and braided with long strips of leather and beads. I saw her bent over the fire, turning the rabbit as she cooked our meal. I envisioned her cleaning buffalo hides. Anything that I could hold on to, to keep in my heart and to pull up at will when I wanted to see her again.

And Father, my dear father, Black Hawk's brave warrior. He would always be etched in my mind…tall, with black hair slick from bear fat. His strong arms could shoot an arrow so straight he would hit his target every time, but gentle when he put them around me.

Will time make my family a faded memory?

Chapter 14

August 9, 1832

Mother Jordan usually awoke first each morning, but not that morning. In my excitement, I was wide awake before the sun came up. Lying beside Amanda, my mind raced, planning how I could be with my sisters once again. With great anticipation, I rehearsed my meeting with them and my speech I would say to Father Jordan. Father Jordan seemed like a good man, and I felt sure he would allow my sisters to live here, too. I knew we could help Mother Jordan fix food, feed the animals, and maybe even help with other things they did around their lodge. It wasn't like our wigwams, but I thought they could show us what to do. We didn't need a box to sleep in. We would even sleep outside. Even Askuwheteau could help with the animals. Once well again, he could go hunting for the family. That would help Father Jordan.

I heard Mother Jordan in the other room as she went about her morning chores. *If I got up to help her, she'd see how much I could do. She'd see for herself that my sisters and I could make things easier for her. Maybe then, she could sit for a spell under one of the trees with Father Jordan when he whittles on his wood pieces. My mother and father sat* together sometimes when they watched the dancers weave their way around the campfire. Once I even saw my father take my mother's hand in his. It wasn't for long, but I saw it. Maybe they were remembering when they were young and danced around the fire.

I eased out from under the covers and walked silently across the cool, rough wood. The door made a scraping sound across the floor as I opened it. Mother Jordan had her back to me but turned when she heard the door. She motioned for me to approach her.

Slowly, I inched my way closer. Like Father Jordan, she had warmth about her. "Athemihiwewa."

Father Jordan opened the door to the lodge. "She wants to help you, Mama. She said, 'Can I help?'"

I looked at him then back to her. I was so glad he understood. "Athemihiwewa."

Father Jordan took my hand. "Help, Katie. Say help. That is what you want to do, isn't it? You want to help Mother Jordan?"

I shook my head. "H-e-l-p."

"See I knew you could say it. Just tell Mother Jordan you want to help."

"Help."

We looked at each other and laughed. I said my first white man's word. Help. When my sisters came to live with us, we'd know what to say.

Father Jordan sat down at the table while Mother Jordan poured a liquid into a cup for him. The steam rose above his head as he brought it up to his face to take a drink. I didn't know what the liquid was, but it smelled good. Perhaps some morning I would have a cup of it, too.

He put his cup down, and I thought I saw sadness in

his eyes when he looked at me. He bowed his head and whispered something. I thought he might be talking to his father like he did when we ate. Someday, I'd have to ask him about this father.

Mother Jordan interrupted my thoughts. She handed me the plates, pointed to the table, and then back to the door where everyone slept.

I looked at Father Jordan. "She said to put the plates on the table then go wake the others."

I placed each plate perfectly on the table for each child. As I laid the last plate in front of Father Jordan, the door to their sleeping room slowly opened. Askuwheteau stood in the doorway looking like he'd slept for days and days. His hair stood out all over his head, and his eyes squinted like he was half asleep. He scratched his chest and yawned.

He stood tall in the doorway, shoulders reaching both sides of the door. I watched him go outside.

"Where are you going?" I called after him.

He turned around and looked at me, then spoke to Father Jordan. "I must leave. It is time."

I ran to him and threw my arms around his waist. "No, no, you can't go. I just found my sisters on the boat. There is a boat here with many of our people on it. Maybe your family is on the boat, too. Please don't go."

"You saw a boat?" He bent down and grabbed my shoulders. "Where did you see this boat?"

This news appeared to bring Askuwheteau fully awake.

Father Jordan stood up and moved beside me. He put his hand on Askuwheteau's shoulder. "There's a boat docked on the river getting ready to leave today to carry the survivors of the massacre down river. I'll take you there after you've eaten something. Like Katie said, maybe your family is on the boat."

Askuwheteau looked at me then back to Father Jordan. "I'll eat, but then I must go and find my people. I don't think my family is on that boat you talk of. Thank you for taking care of me, but I cannot stay."

"That's all I can ask of you," Father Jordan continued. "You're welcome to stay as long as you want. I don't think your wounds have healed enough for you to travel. But, if that is what you want to do, then I can't stop you."

The small cabin filled with chatter as the children came into the room and each one sat down to the table. Father Jordan bowed his head as he had done in the past. Askuwheteau sat next to me watching everything.

I took his hand and whispered. "You have to put your head down so Father Jordan can talk to his father."

Askuwheteau looked at me, Father Jordan, then back to me.

The baffled look on his face made me want to laugh. I could only imagine what he was thinking. My thoughts raced to the boat, my sisters, my parents, and how much help my sisters and I were going to be for Mother Jordan. I was too excited to eat anything.

Chapter 15

August 9, 1832

Father Jordan walked several steps in front of Askuwheteau and me, occasionally turning to see how far back we were. "Come along you two so we can get to the boat before it leaves."

Askuwheteau and I were eager to get to the boat before its long trip down river. We had to look for his people, and to take my sisters off. *How will I ask Father Jordan if we can all stay with him?* My stomach churned.

Words tumbled over and over in my head practicing what I would say. *Father Jordan please let my sisters stay with me. We are strong and we can help you and Mother Jordan. Please let my sisters stay with your family too. We are all strong and can work like any man. We can do our share. You will not be sorry if you let us all stay.* I decided that would never do. *Father Jordan, Mother Jordan needs help around your lodge. Please let my sisters stay with me so we can keep your lodge clean, cook your meals, and take care of your animals.*

In the distance, I saw smoke billowing above the place where the boat rested. I heard voices coming from that direction too. I started to run. "Hurry."

My breath fell in short gasps as I reached the dock. Askuwheteau was right behind me. I scanned the faces along the railing looking for my sisters. They were nowhere in sight. I prayed "Please let them be there." *Isn't that what Father Jordan did every time we sat down to eat. How funny of me to remember that now.*

I paced back and forth looking, searching each face for a familiar one. The wail of the ship's whistle startled me. Fear gripped me from the bottom of my stomach and rumbled through my body. "No. No...Please don't leave." I turned to Father Jordan. "Don't let them leave, please, don't let them leave yet. I have to see my sisters. I have to go with them."

Father Jordan picked me up.

"Please let me go to them. I have to see them. Maybe they can stay here. That's it; they can stay here. With me. With all of us."

"I'm afraid they can't stay here, Katie. They have to go with the boat. Go aboard and see them one more time. I'll talk to Captain Throckmorton. Askuwheteau has already gone aboard to see if his family is there. Run along."

My feet became like hoofs of deer. They barely touched the ground as I ran across the dirt and over the ramp to get on board the boat. I took the steps two at a time to get to the second deck. When I reached the top, there were so many faces, all within the reach of my hands. But none of them were my sisters. I ran in and out of the throngs of people calling their names. No answer.

Finally, I spotted Ootadabun, towering above the others on the other side of the deck. Sokanon and Ootadabun leaned against the rail facing me. They looked so sad. I wanted to run to them, but something in their faces told me what my heart already knew. They were going without me. I bolted toward them crying. "I want to go with you. I have to go with you. Please don't leave me."

We huddled together crying. Tears burned my cheeks as they streamed down to the corners of my mouth. It tasted salty as I licked my lips. I couldn't talk. No one could. My heart was being torn from my chest once more. All thoughts of Askuwheteau and Father Jordan vanished, only the thoughts of my own family remained. *A family torn apart from war. The white man's war.*

Ootadabun gave me a hug then pushed me from her. "Listen to me. You must stay here with your new family. You cannot go with us. I heard some of the older ones talking last night. The place they are taking us is not good. Others have gone before us and many have died. You have a chance at life here. You must take it. Be strong."

"I don't want to be here without you. I cannot bear the thought of me here and you gone to wherever they are taking you. No. I will not stay." I planted my feet on the floor and crossed my arms looking at my sisters with defiance.

Sokanon spun me around and bent down eye level with me. "I will not hear of your talk any more. You will listen to us, and you will do as we say. You will stay here. We do not know of the danger that lies before us. Stay here and learn the white man's ways. Be one step ahead of him. Think of our mother and our father. Be strong for them. Someday, maybe, our paths will cross again."

I could feel my resistance weaken. More tears welled up within me and started spilling. "You're my family. You're all I have. I cannot stay without you."

The long low blast of the whistle made me tremble. This was not my plan. "Wait, I'll talk to Father Jordan, and he'll let you stay with me. He's a good man. He wouldn't make you go away." With those words, I turned and ran to the stairs. Surely, I could make them stop the boat and let my sisters off.

Askuwheteau and I jumped off the boat at the same time. "Did you find your family?"

"No. Did you find your sisters?"

"Yes, but I must talk to Father Jordan quickly."

I spotted Father Jordan, waving to me to hurry up. My feet flew. "Father Jordan, Father Jordan. Don't let the boat leave."

When I reached his open arms, I bounded into them just like the first time I saw him. "Father Jordan, please let my sisters stay here with us. We can help Mother Jordan with your lodge and with your animals. Please let them stay." The words tumbled out before I could think of exactly what I wanted to say.

He grabbed my head tenderly and laid it on his shoulder. "My dear child, we cannot take them off the boat. They have to go down river to the white man's fort. I've already talked to Captain Throckmorton, and he agrees. You're to stay here with my family and me. You cannot help your sisters now."

I struggled to get out of his arms, but the more I struggled, the tighter he gripped me. If I could only get down, I would run and jump aboard before anyone could stop me. My plan was not working out the way I wanted it to. If my sisters left now, I knew I would never see them again.

The whistle blew again, and I watched as the men untied the ropes holding the boat to the boards on the dock. People cried, wailing in my language. *Why? Why won't they let my people off the boat? From the time the fighting started until now, my people have been killed, reduced to so few. Now the white man has herded my sisters and my people like the great buffalo and penned them up on a boat to take them to who knows where.*

Even though my sisters didn't say so, I felt they knew what was going to happen once they arrived at the fort. After the fort, their fate was in the white man's hands. In my heart, I vowed that I would go to the white man's fort and look for my sisters when I was older. I would find them.

Through tears, my sisters faded from my sight. Other faces became one big blur. With determination, I promised myself I would find them someday. I laid my head on Father Jordan's shoulder and softly cried as the boat slowly drifted down river. My chest ached while the sound of water slapping against the boat faded. Father Jordan turned around and headed back to his lodge. Askuwheteau followed, dragging his feet.

We reached the lodge mid-morning. Father Jordan walked over to his favorite chair sitting against the outside of the lodge and sat down, still holding me. In my short time living in their lodge, I watched Father Jordan as he sat in this chair as he carved things out of small pieces of wood. Once, he carved a spoon for Mother Jordan, so she could stir food in the big pot she used every day.

Askuwheteau stopped in front of Father Jordan. "Thank you, but since my family was not on the boat, I must leave now to find them."

Father Jordan stood up and sat me down in the chair. He grabbed Askuwheteau by his shoulders. "You don't have to leave. Surely, you could stay a few more days to get your strength back. Katie has a home here with our family, and you're welcome to stay, too."

"No, I cannot. I've been here too long. Memekeha, Katie as you call her, will be fine here with you, but I must leave. Some of the people on the boat said they thought my father made it across the river. I must see if I can find him. I am strong enough."

Father Jordan crossed his arm to his chest and back to Askuwheteau. "I understand. Let me give you food for your journey and a blanket to keep you warm. You have your knife to keep you safe. What else can I get for you?"

"You have done enough. I will remember you in the winter of my life and how you took care of me."

Father Jordan turned and walked to the barn.

When I looked into Askuwheteau's eyes, my heart sank still lower. "No!"

He knelt down to me and took both hands in his. "Memekeha, you know I must do this. I must find my people. Father Jordan will take care of you as if you were his own daughter. I am sure of it. Who knows, I may come back to visit you sometime."

There were no more tears. They were all gone. Only the hole in my heart remained. Everyone I knew and loved had left me and now my last friend was leaving. It was more than I could bear. "Why can't I go with you? I won't be any trouble. I'll help you."

"No, you cannot go with me again. You have a new family here. They'll take care of you. They'll feed you and show you how to cook; you will learn to make your own clothes, and everything else there is to know about growing up. You'll have a long life. I know this."

All I could do was watch him as Father Jordan put a blanket around his shoulders and gave him a pouch with provisions. With each step he took away from me, pieces of my heart continued to break. He never looked back. I sat riveted to the chair, frozen, the last piece of my life disappearing into the brush.

Chapter 16

September 15, 1832

As each day drifted by, my family grew dimmer in my mind. Days turned into weeks. I stopped counting how many times the new moon's light showed through the cracks and windows of our lodge.

When I closed my eyes at night, I saw my sisters wave goodbye to me. When I awoke, the same visions were still present; I wondered where my mother and father were. My heart told me they lived with the Great Spirit, but I didn't want to believe it. I wanted to think that someday I would see them again. *Someday, they will come walking up to Father Jordan's lodge with outstretched arms ready to take me with them.*

It's not that Father Jordan wasn't a good father or that Mother Jordan didn't teach me her ways. I just wanted my own father and mother to put me to bed each night, to wrap me in my blanket like they used to.

Thoughts of my friend, Askuwheteau, looking for his family crept into my mind, too. How far will he travel before he finds his people? Did he find them yet? I'll probably never know.

One morning, after we had eaten our meal, Father

Jordan looked at me with his tender, laughing eyes. "Katie, how would you like to go with me to the pond and see if we can catch some fish for our dinner? I think Mother Jordan would like to have a batch of fish to fry up for tonight's meal." He turned to Mother Jordan and winked. "Wouldn't you, my dear? And I saw Samuel finished his chores early this morning, so he will go with us. Would you like that, Katie?"

Mother Jordan smiled and nodded her head. "You run along, Katie. It'll probably do you some good to be out in the fresh air. You've been moping around the house far too long. Run along. I'll take care of the dishes."

Between Mother Jordan, Samuel, and Amanda, I learned the white man's language. There were times when Samuel and I sat behind the barn as he taught me easy words. I still had trouble, but in the end, I understood what they were trying to say. In turn, everyone else learned my language. Sometimes not as well as I learned theirs.

Fishing? And with Samuel too? Many times Samuel came to my aid when I couldn't figure out how to do something. He taught me how to tie knots with the lead rope we used to steer the cows back to the barn. Samuel always seemed to know when I felt like crying. Like a medicine man, he showed up at just the right time to wipe away my tears. He had me laughing before I knew it. Now he was going to fish with Father Jordan and me. The thought of my father taking my brothers fishing came to mind. I never got to go with them. I guess it was because I was a girl, not a warrior like them. Before anyone could change their minds, I jumped out of my chair and raced out the door.

The sun felt warm on my face as I sat beside Father Jordan on the bank of the pond. He threw his line far into the water and gave the pole a jerk; "Now keep an eye on the reed."

I watched as the reed settled upon the still water. Father Jordan pointed to it. "When the floater disappears under the water, I know the fish has taken the bait on the hook; I set it by, jerking the pole. Then I pull him in."

My brothers had talked about how they caught fish, but not with a pole and floater. They waded into the river and watched as the fish swam around their feet; then with their arrows, they speared the fish. Yes, the white man does have different ways.

I watched Samuel as he followed Father Jordan's actions and threw his line out into the water. His pale yellow hair blew slightly in the breeze as he sat down with his pole. The silence gave way to my mind wandering, drifting back to not so long ago. How could so much happen in such a short time? My life went from living with my father and mother to living with a white family. They aren't so different, I guess. They just do things differently. I lived in a lodge with my family. The white people live in a cabin, that I still call their lodge. My family all slept together in our blankets and robes. This family sleeps in boxes with their blankets. My mother cooked our meals over open campfires, while this family cooks their meals in their lodge, and they eat off dishes. That's what Mother Jordan calls them. And I have to wash them after the meals. This family takes baths in a big tub with hot water at least once a week. We jumped into the river whenever we wanted. That is, the ones that could swim. I waded close to shore. We didn't consider it taking a bath, just playing in the water. In my heart, I knew I would never see my family again. This was my new home and family now.

The water glistened from the sun reaching high overhead. I patted the dry dirt beside me and began to draw circles, then birds, our lodges, and connected them with lines, and more lines.

"Katie, look, the floater is gone," Father Jordan shouted. "Perhaps we have a fish for dinner?"

I jumped up to see if Father Jordan had indeed caught a fish. He began pulling the line into shore. I saw the fish come to the surface then disappear below the water again.

"Can I help?" I ran toward the pole. "Can I pull the line, too?"

Father Jordan motioned me toward the line, and we both pulled. "Samuel, come help Katie pull the line." I just knew we'd caught the biggest fish in the pond, enough for all of us to eat that night. As Father Jordan gave the pole one last tug, the fish came ashore, flopping around in the dirt.

Father Jordan began to laugh. "Well, Katie, it isn't the biggest fish in the pond, but it will do. Guess we need to put it on our string until we can catch some more to make a good meal for dinner. Samuel, look, I think you have one, too. Quick, grab your pole."

I watched Samuel give his pole a jerk. When he did, the fish flew out of the water onto the ground. I laughed as the fish flopped like the other one did on dry land. We all laughed.

"Now we have two for dinner." Father Jordan said.

Father Jordan carefully put the string through the fish's mouth then through its gills, then lay both in the water with a rock holding the string." Wouldn't want him to swim away now, would we?"

After he sat down on the bank, he and Samuel, in

unison, pulled a worm from a can between them, and began squishing it together on the hook. It wiggled about, probably knowing what lay ahead of him, as they strung him on the hook. Together they threw their lines and floater back into the pond to await another fish. We sat down together and watched as the reed landed out in the water and settled down.

"Father Jordan," I said. "Can I ask you something?"

He ran his hand through my hair. "Of course you can, child. What have you been thinking, Katie?"

"Well, I was wondering, am I going to live with you for the rest of my life now? I really miss my mother and father, but I don't think they are coming for me. Do you?"

He sat silent for a few minutes. I wondered if he was going to answer me. "Katie, you're very young to understand a lot of things, but you've been through quite a lot for your age. No, child, I don't think they'll be coming for you. As for staying with Mother Jordan and me, well, we want you to stay. You're part of our family now, and you'll always have a home with us." He put his arm around my shoulder, and for the first time in a very long time, I felt warm inside. And I felt wanted.

We sat in peaceful silence. I didn't want this moment to end. Someone wanted to take care of me. He wanted me to call him, Father. I glanced up to see Father Jordan looking out over the water. His eyes seemed fixed on the small reed dancing on the water. My guess was that he wanted to be able to snag another fish the minute the floater disappeared. It was late afternoon when we headed back to the cabin.

We heard Amanda calling Father Jordan's name before we saw her. She skipped toward us. "Mother asked me to come out and give you a hand. She knew you'd need extra help to carry your big catch back home." She giggled and grabbed the string of flopping fish. "By the looks of this, you could have handled it just fine." She grinned and looked at Samuel. "Samuel, I guess you let ole' muddy get away again."

I watched Samuel's face redden and wondered what Amanda was saying. *I would have to ask him what she meant when we were alone.*

"Pa, Samuel stacked the wood like you asked him to, and Andrew cleaned the barn and the pig pens." Amanda rattled on without catching her breath. "Do you think everyone could go into town this Saturday with you and maybe get a bag of peppermint sticks?" She held the fish up in the air and ran her finger down each one.

Father Jordan looked at me and back to Amanda. "Well, now, I do have to get some feed at the feed store, and I'm sure Momma could buy some new calico for a dress or two. Have you done all your chores?"

Amanda looked up at Father Jordan and smiled. "Yes, Pa, I have." Her long lashes fluttered as she spoke.

"Well, then, I'll talk to Mama when we get home. Maybe, just maybe, it's to town with everyone this Saturday."

We cleaned our catch of ten fish for the evening meal. *Mother Jordan will be so proud of us, plenty of fish for everyone to eat their fill.*

After dinner, we lingered at the table talking. Everyone was eager to go to town and pick out their own peppermint candy stick. *Another thing, I'll have to ask Samuel is what peppermint is.* Even Mother Jordan began making plans of what cloth to buy and who needed a new dress. I hadn't been to town yet, so I didn't know what to expect. *Was it like going to the fort and exchanging my father's furs for blankets?* The more we talked, the more excited I became. The family had much to do to get ready before our journey in two days.

"Father Jordan, how far is it to town?"

"It's about a two hour ride. We'll leave early, after the animals are fed. Right now, I think it's getting late. Off to bed with all of you. You've had a full day around here."

No one even grumbled about going to bed that night. I think everyone had thoughts of what they were going to see in town in two days, maybe even what they were going to buy. I knew Samuel and Andrew earned money when they worked for the farm down the road. I saw them give their money to Mother Jordan. She put it in the big red jar that sat on the highest shelf over the worktable in the kitchen. I had seen Father Jordan put money in the same jar after he helped wagons cross the river on his ferry.

Long after everyone had fallen asleep, I lay awake staring at the ceiling wondering what I was going to see in town. Bear lay between Amanda and me with his head across my stomach. I ran my hand over his fur several times. Every time I stopped, he took his paw and laid it on my hand. *Oh, Bear, do you know what I'm thinking? Sometimes I think you do, especially when you sit by me when I start thinking of my mother and father. You seem to sense when I feel like crying for my family, for me, for the life I will never live again.*

These walls were the walls of my lodge now. This family was my new family. Their ways were my ways from this time on. Bear raised his head.

The Jordan family had been good to me, but it still wasn't like my own mother and father, my own sisters and brothers. I would never see my brother shoot arrows again or watch with him behind trees as the arrow found its mark. Then running with him to make sure his kill was dead, ready to skin, and divide the meat up for our families. He was so proud of his kills and was ready to take the last rites to become a warrior like our father. I vowed to do better about not thinking of my family, to push them to a safer place in my mind, to give them to the Great Spirit.

Chapter 17

September 17, 1832

My feet flew over the side of the bed as I threw the blanket over Amanda's face. I grabbed my dress, and heard Amanda's muffled voice from under the blanket, "Katie, what are you doing?"

My fingers franticly tied the ribbons on my dress; I was almost to the door. Whispering so not to wake everyone, "I want to be ready for when we leave for town."

The sun barely peeked through the window. I wanted to surprise Mother Jordan and have the table all set for everyone by the time she got up to fix the morning meal. Slowly, I opened the door and to my surprise, Mother Jordan was standing at the fireplace stirring something in the pot. She turned when she heard the door open.

"My dear child, I knew you'd be too excited to sleep late. Go wash your face and comb your hair. I have your oatmeal ready for you. And when you're finished you can help load the wagon for our trip. Now run along." She smiled and pointed to the door. "I'll get everyone else up so they can help."

I didn't need much encouragement as I skipped out the door and over to the bucket of fresh water. It was cold as

I splashed it over my face, but I did as I was told. I ran back inside and sat down eating without taking a breath. The sooner I ate, the sooner we could get the wagon going into town. I thought back to the time I first came here. I didn't remember the Jordan family going into town before, but sometimes Andrew left for a long period of time, then returned with packages. The packages were filled with sewing thread for Mother Jordan, nails for Father Jordan, and other items. Maybe he went to town by himself to get supplies. It seemed like there was always so much to do around the house that there was no time for trips, especially to town. Now we were going, and I was going to go, too.

. . .

Once the family settled in for the ride, Father Jordan headed the wagon toward the river. "Today, we'll take the ferry across and go to East Dubuque, the big city, on the other side of the river. This is a special day, Katie's first day to go to town." He gave the reins a tug, and the mule gave the wagon a jerk, sending me backwards into Samuel's lap. Everyone laughed.

A short distance from the house lay the mighty river with Father Jordan's ferry. As he pulled the wagon to a stop, Andrew and Samuel jumped out. "Looks like the river has risen, Pa," shouted Andrew. "Must be from rains to the north."

"That could be, son. Everyone stay in the wagon until we get on the ferry. Then the boys will pull us over to the other side."

Father Jordan led the mule aboard the flat boat. Then Andrew unhooked the line to the shore and steered us across the river from the line above. From the back of the ferry, I watched the river slowly flow; making its way down the same way the big boat went when it took my sisters to the fort. I wondered if they were already there.

"We're about there," Samuel shouted. "Come up here with me, Katie, and see the city."

I ran to the front of the ferry. "Look at the tall lodges. They do not look like your lodge."

Father Jordan followed me. He put his hand on my shoulder and laughed. "No, Katie, they are not lodges; they are stores—stores to buy food, stores to buy building materials and stores to buy whatever you need. Andrew, throw the line so we can tie up."

"Yes, Pa," Andrew replied. He threw the rope to a man standing on the wooden dock waiting to tie up the ferry.

After Samuel and Andrew unloaded the fresh eggs from the wagon, we began our short walk down the street. I couldn't stop looking at all the people. Two men rode horses with pelts piled high behind their saddles. Young boys kicked a ball down the dusty street. I saw two old men sitting on a porch step smoking pipes. Women and children dressed in fine clothing strolled past us. I wore my pretty dress Mother Jordan had given me.

Mother Jordan pointed to a sign above a building. "Come along, we're going to buy some cloth to make new dresses. I think the boys could use new shirts, too."

As the door swung open, I saw two women standing by a high table looking at cloth. One was tall with her hair pulled straight back into a bun on top of her head. The other was shorter, older looking, and hair as black as night.

Behind them, colors of red, yellow, and blue fabric lined the walls. An older man wearing glasses stood behind the table helping the women decide which cloth to buy. When we walked in, they all stopped talking and looked our way.

"Good morning, Mr. Goodnight," Mother Jordan said with a smile. "I've brought my girls to pick out some of your fine cloth to make new dresses. By the looks of all the dry goods, I'd say you've received a new shipment."

The man waved. "Yes, Mrs. Jordan, we received the shipment just a day ago. I'm sure you'll find what you're looking for."

The two women turned and smiled at Mother Jordan; their smiles faded as they looked at each of the girls and stopped at me. They turned back to the man and bent together saying something I couldn't hear.

Amanda took me by the arm and steered me to the corner of the store and showed me cloth she called gingham. "Look, Katie, look at this one. Keep looking and find the color you like the best. I'm going to ask Mother if I can have two bolts."

I ran my hand over the bright flowers. The cloth felt soft on my skin. My fingers traced each petal. It reminded me of my sister who liked to pick the flowers along the river and bring them to Mother. Small yellow blossoms covered this cloth Amanda called calico.

When I turned around to find Mother Jordan, I saw the two women looking at me again. I walked over to Mother Jordan. Both women yelled at me. I stopped in my tracks and stood still, wondering what I had done. Mother Jordan said something to them. Their hands flew to their mouths at the same time. The tall woman walked toward Mother Jordan saying something, and the tone of her voice frightened me. I didn't understand. I could tell it was not good. Elsie and I stood behind Mother Jordan, both of us peering out from the back of her skirt. The tall woman bent down and looked me right in the eye. Her face almost touched my nose. She said something again. Her face reddened, and she began to yell. Mother Jordan said something, and the tall woman stopped, looked Mother Jordan in the face, turned, grabbed the shorter woman by the arm, and walked out the door.

The man, Mr. Goodnight, looked pale. He said something to Mother Jordan while straightening the cloth. He lowered his head while Mother Jordan paid for her purchase with the money Father Jordan put in the red jar. *This must be the way they buy their supplies. Not like my people when we go to the fort and trade furs for supplies. Someday, I will know more words and ways of the white people. I wonder what those women said to Mother Jordan.*

At the end of the day, we gathered at the boat to take our wagon full of purchases back across the river to our lodge. With the excitement of the day, little conversation happened until we reached our lodge, unloaded the wagon, and gathered at the table for bread and cheese before turning in for the night.

When I finally lay down beside Amanda, I rolled toward her. "What did those women say to me in the store? They sounded like they were angry."

"I wouldn't worry about it, Katie. Some people just don't like Indians, no matter what. Go to sleep." She rolled over and brought the covers up to her shoulders.

I didn't understand, but I would ask Father Jordan tomorrow. He would know.

The next morning before everyone gathered at the table, I asked Father Jordan about what had happened the day before. "Did you hear about the women in the store? Do you know what they said to me? It sounded like they were angry with me."

Father Jordan took my hand and led me around the table. "Hop up here, young lady." He patted his lap. I eagerly climbed up. "Some people do not understand the Indian ways. They think they all want to fight. Many white people think the color of the Indian's skin means they're all savages who want to kill them. They're afraid of what they don't know. Because you have darker skin doesn't say what kind of person you are." It looked like he had water in his eyes when he spoke to me. "Some think that all Indians are bad only because they do not take the time to know them. They don't know you, Katie. You are a child, not responsible for the actions of your people. You're responsible for your actions and yours alone. I pray each day that you won't be faced with the mean ways of some people. There are many good people out there, like Mother Jordan and myself, who know you for who you are."

"Does that mean I can't go into town anymore?"

He put his arms around me. "No, no, Katie. It doesn't mean that. It means we have to give it time; time for others to see you for who you are. Patience, my dear Katie, patience."

I jumped down and sat at my place at the table. *Someday, I will know this word patience. Someday.*

Chapter 18

March 1833

It seemed like a long time ago when we took the trip to the big city, but Father Jordan said only six months had passed. Now he decided he was going to take Andrew and Samuel into town with him to pick up supplies for Mother Jordan, plus nails to fix the barn and fences. The ones he pulled out of the old fence couldn't be straightened anymore and some even fell apart. I'm glad I didn't have to go, as I didn't want to see those two women again, not anytime soon anyway.

Father Jordan left early that morning for Flat Rock, only three miles away. As he hitched the mule to the wagon, he said, "I'll get the supplies I need, and I'll be home quicker than going to Dubuque, and hopefully before the storm rolls in."

I looked up at the sky and wondered how he knew there would be a storm. The sun shined over the trees and the day felt warm already. Almost too warm, like it wanted to rain, but the heat wouldn't let it. The air stood still, not a breeze blowing. Maybe a summer storm would cool the air. My grandfather could always tell when a storm was coming. Maybe Father Jordan and grandfather knew something I didn't.

I waved as Father Jordan headed the wagon away from the lodge. Samuel turned around and waved back. "We'll be home soon, Katie."

I watched until the wagon drove out of sight, then I headed toward the lodge to help with canning. Mother Jordan talked about canning vegetables and said I would need to learn these things for later, when I married and had a family of my own. I would be able to feed them through the long winter months. That seemed so far off to me. My mother had always dried meat to last us through the cold snow laden months.

. . .

Even though it was still afternoon, the sky looked darker than usual. The wind had gathered speed for the last hour leaving Mother Jordan, Amanda, and myself scrambling to pick up anything that blew away. Elsie joined us, picking up what we dropped from our packed arms.

It was late when Father Jordan pulled the wagon into the yard. Samuel jumped down from the wagon and unhooked the mule before leading him to the barn. The door flew out of his hands and hit the side of the barn with a loud bang. Father Jordan and Andrew pushed the wagon alongside the barn to get it out of the way.

"Get in the cabin." Father Jordan's words were muffled by the wind. To make sure we understood, he pointed to the lodge.

The wind blew with tremendous force by the time we made it to the lodge and tried to close the door. Before I entered, I turned around and called out for Samuel. He was nowhere in sight. Father Jordan grabbed my arm and pulled me inside holding the door open. I bent down peering between his legs, then spotted Samuel running toward the cabin. Father Jordan yelled, "Come on, son. Get in here."

Just before Samuel reached the door, I heard a loud crack and watched as a large branch from a tree blew across his back, knocking him down face first. Father Jordan ran out, picked him up, and carried him back to the lodge. Mother Jordan pushed the door closed while the wind howled against the sides of the cabin. The wind roared and swirled so quickly that I thought the roof would fly off. I had heard these winds before when we lived out on the plains while the warriors were buffalo hunting. Those winds lifted our lodges off the ground never to be found again. I started to shake.

Father Jordan lay Samuel's small frame on his bed while Mother Jordan gathered cloth and water to wash the blood from his face. I raced over to see if I could help.

"He'll be all right, Katie. It looks like a scrape, a few bruises; he'll be all right." Mother Jordan brushed the dirt from his forehead. "Oh my, it does look like his head may have hit a rock when he fell. It appears to be deeper than I thought."

"Please, may I get him some water? More cloth?" I wanted to help.

I turned to get some water, but Father Jordan handed me the cup already filled. "Here, Katie, give this to him."

I handed the water to Samuel.

He smiled. "Aww, Katie, I'm not hurt. It's just a scratch."

Mother Jordan laughed. "Just like a man. It's just a scratch. True, Samuel, it may be a scratch, but let us baby you for now."

Samuel's face reddened. The wind got louder. Something

hit the side of the cabin, then another loud bang. Father Jordan knelt down by Samuel's bed. "Come on, everyone, get over here together. Mama, you and Samuel get on the floor, too. Stay together and keep your heads down."

Father Jordan bowed his head and the others followed his lead. "Father, watch over us and keep us safe through this storm."

There he goes again talking to his father. Someday I'm going to ask him who and where his father is.

We sat there all night leaning against each other. Early the next morning, I awoke leaning against Andrew's shoulder. Light began peeking through the crack in the door. Everything was quiet. No one else was awake yet. Father Jordan sat against the bed with his arm around Mother Jordan; their heads leaned against each other. Amanda slept with her head on Father Jordan's lap and Elsie's curled body had her head resting on Mother Jordan's lap. Samuel's head lay on Andrew's lap. I heard the mule bray.

Father Jordan sat up straight and rubbed his neck. "Oh, my neck is stiff." He laid Mother Jordan's head back against the bed, placed Amanda's head on Mother Jordan's lap, and slowly stood up. I stood up, too.

Together we slipped out of the sleeping room. I whispered. "I don't hear the wind now."

Father Jordan headed toward the door with me right behind him. "I don't hear anything right now either. Let's take a look outside." He slowly pulled the door open.

Under grey, gloomy skies, we saw tree branches strewn all over the ground. The barn door hung on one hinge. At least the wind had stopped, and it wasn't raining.

"It's a good thing we picked up everything that was

loose before taking shelter, but it still looks like there is much to clean up," I whispered.

Even with all of us, except Samuel, working from morning till evening, it took three days to clean all the loose brush and tree limbs scattered around the lodge. Father Jordan fixed the barn door and replaced the poles on the fences that had blown down. When he came into the lodge that night, Samuel, still in bed from his injury, said he was tired and felt worse. The cut on his head appeared bright red. When Samuel came to the table to eat, he barely touched anything.

I waited until we were ready to go to bed before I asked Father Jordan about him. "Is Samuel going to be all right? He didn't eat any of his meal tonight."

Father Jordan said, "I'm sure he's fine. He's probably just weary from lying in bed the last few days."

Late into the night, after we had all gone to bed, I lay quietly, listening to everyone breathing, their tossing and turning, and murmuring in their sleep. I sat up between Amanda and Elsie and looked toward Samuel, lying across the room from me, as he moaned and tossed from side to side. I slipped out of bed and tip toed to his side. Sitting on the floor beside him, I took his hand. It felt hot, very hot. Mother Jordan found me there when she came to check on Samuel early the next morning.

"Goodness, child. Why are you sitting here?" She took my hand from Samuel's and felt his face. "Katie, go get a pan of water."

I headed for the big room to get a pan of water. No one else stirred yet. By the time I came back, Mother Jordan was brushing Samuel's hair back from his face. His eyes were closed, and he looked white—white like the clouds on a summer day. My stomach knotted. I handed the pan to Mother Jordan.

"Child, can you get a cloth to wash his face?"

"Yes, Mother Jordan. Is he going to be all right?" Before she could answer, I was off again to the big room to look for the cloth she had put by the water pail the night before. I grabbed it and headed back to the sleeping room. As I handed it to her, I fell at her feet and sat waiting for her to work her medicine on Samuel. His moaning remained low as he tossed his head back and forth. Mother Jordan put his hands under the blanket and began wiping his face with the wet cloth. The cut on his head looked different. Instead of a dark reddish color, it appeared puffy with white stuff oozing from the corners. Mother Jordan wiped his face. I watched Samuel's every move.

The first light of gray dawn started to fill the room when I heard Amanda's voice behind me. I turned to see her holding Elsie's hand. Both looked scared. "Mother, is Samuel going to be all right? What's wrong?"

"It looks like the cut on his forehead is infected, dear. Will you please take Katie and Elsie into the other room and fix them something to eat. Papa and Andrew. Samuel will be just fine. Now run along."

Amanda reached for me, but I slid closer to Samuel. "No, please, Mother Jordan, I want to stay here with you."

"Nonsense, child, run along with Amanda." Mother Jordan leaned down, pushed my hair back away from my face, and kissed my forehead. "Samuel's going to be fine. Father Jordan will need your help with the animals, and so will Andrew. You can come back as soon as your chores are finished."

I stood up and slowly walked backward toward the door

watching Samuel's every movement. I had seen that oozing white stuff before when warriors had been wounded. It was not good for them and now I wondered if it would be the same for Samuel. My heart hurt for my friend. *Great Spirit take care of him. Hold him in your great hands. Isn't that what Father Jordan would ask when he talks to his father?*

By the time we finished feeding the animals, gathering the eggs, and eating the morning meal, the sun radiated high above. The air felt warm against my skin as I shook out the blanket from my bed. Mother Jordan said that if we shook our blankets each day, they would feel light and smell fresh when we pulled them up against our chins at night. This was something new to me. My mother always left our blankets on the ground for us to lie on each night. But I did think Mother Jordan was right; it did smell fresh.

When I spread my blanket on the bed, my gaze went directly over to Samuel. He lay so still. No one else was in the room, so I slowly made my way over to him. No sounds came from him, not even a sigh. My heart froze, afraid to venture any further. I stood watching Samuel, waiting for him to say something, to move, or to moan. Slowly I crept toward his bed, my eyes fixed on his sleeping face. When I reached him, my trembling hand stretched out to touch his hand. He didn't move. I jerked my hand back. Again, I grasped his hand. When he didn't move again, I shook him. "Samuel." I whispered. He didn't respond. He didn't move. I stood beside him watching. There was nothing. "Eeyyyyiiiiiiii."

I felt Father Jordan's hands on my shoulders. My shoulders shook with sobs. "Noooo." *This can't be happening. He can't leave me, too.* "Father Jordan, please, is Samuel all right?" I wrenched myself free from Father

Jordan's grip and threw myself on Samuel's bed. "Don't let him leave me."

Before he could answer, the room filled with Mother Jordan, Amanda, Andrew, and Elsie. Everyone talked at once, but I couldn't make out anything over my own crying.

Mother Jordan ran her hand over Samuel's face, and then shook him. She too, cried. "Papa, my baby boy is gone."

Father Jordan took her in his arms to comfort her. Her sobs became louder. Elsie and Amanda stood beside Samuel with blank faces.

Why aren't they crying? I cried for my friend. My heart felt like it was breaking into little pieces and falling into a great black hole. I thought it would never be whole again.

Two days later the family buried Samuel in a small hole in the ground not far from their lodge. I watched them place Samuel's wrapped body in the ground and throw dirt over him. The ceremony seemed similar to what my people did with our dead ones. However, we put them in burial mounds, and the loved ones darkened their faces with charcoal and fasted. I remembered going to the mounds with Mother so she could talk to her mother. I often wondered if her mother heard what she said to her.

Father Jordan placed a large piece of wood in the ground with Samuel's name on it. I saw a couple more pieces of wood with names on them not far from Samuel's. Father Jordan told me later that his parents lay in the ground by Samuel.

People came to comfort the family. Father Jordan called them friends who lived nearby and knew Samuel. As we stood together, Father Jordan and everyone else closed their eyes while he said something to his father again. I still had not asked him why he kept talking to his father when I didn't see anyone else there.

Later that night, when Mother Jordan came to my bed to say good night, I asked her why Samuel had to leave. She said the infection ate away at his body. He had been a sickly boy all his life, and the infection was more than his body could overcome. That was all she said. She looked tired and very sad.

Chapter 19

November 1833

The snow came early. Father Jordan said it was time to give thanks to their Father for safety and for all the good things that had happened to their family. Mother Jordan prepared foods like I'd never seen before. I tried to remind myself what each dish was called. There were pumpkin pies, apple breads, corn pone, squash, and mashed potatoes. Never before had I seen so much food at one time, and so many people. Father Jordan said Phoebe and her family from Iowa would make the trip home and stay until the end of the year. Amanda said she had two other sisters, but she didn't talk about them very much. She said Phoebe was four years older than she was and Diana was six. *I remember my sisters; I miss them.*

It's been only four moons since Samuel left. How can they say thank you for that? I couldn't remember how long ago Askuwheteau left me. It felt like yesterday, but then again, it felt like so very long ago.

My heart still hurt for the loss of my mother, father, Askuwheteau, and now for Samuel. I vowed not to let anyone get close to me again. If I didn't let them get close, then when they left, it wouldn't hurt so much. I wondered if the hurting would ever stop.

Mother Jordan smiled as she went about cooking. Even Father Jordan seemed to walk on air as he fed the animals and cleaned the barn. He said the boys would sleep in the barn and the girls in the cabin once they all arrived. There just wouldn't be room for everyone inside.

• • •

The big day came. Phoebe arrived with her husband and two children. Then John. I knew I'd never remember all their names and their children too. When each one arrived, they jumped down from their wagons. Children ran to each other, hugging and laughing. Mother Jordan ran from the cabin with arms outstretched ready to give each one a hug. Father Jordan's laugh preceded his arrival from the barn. His arms raised above his head ready for his embrace.

The feeling of being all alone overwhelmed me as I sat in my shaded spot under the big tree. As much as I felt like a part of their methawihka, it gave me the advantage of watching the family as they sought each other. They seemed eager to embrace one another. The men laughed, slapped each other on their backs, and cheered when they saw how much each child had grown. It looked like they really liked each other. Our clan members greeted one another differently after a long separation. The Indian children ran about and laughed, but our elders were more solemn, almost stone-faced.

As soon as everyone greeted each other, the children took food from the wagon into the lodge. Blankets went to the barn for the boys' beds. The flitting about of everyone reminded me of bees buzzing about flowers then flying back to their hives to deposit the nectar.

Mother Jordan had been cooking food for three days, and now the family brought more food. I thought no one would have to cook again for a very long time.

I still sat under the tree when Amanda came to find me. "So there you are. Mother said she needs you to come help with the food. Everyone helps."

Hesitantly, I stood up and followed her. "Amanda, I don't know your family, only you." With each step, my stomach tightened. "Do you think they will like me?"

She turned. "Don't be silly, Katie. Of course they'll like you." She took my hand and led me toward the lodge. "How could they not like you? I like you."

I pulled my hand from Amanda's and stopped walking.

Amanda looked at me. "Now, what's wrong, Katie?"

"I'm afraid they will look at me like those two women did in the store."

Amanda took my hand again. This time her grip was firm. "Katie, come on. Stop wasting your time with these silly thoughts. My sisters want to meet you."

I heard laughter coming from the lodge. It stopped as soon as I stepped inside the door. I froze. Mother Jordan turned around when the room got quiet She smiled and motioned for me to come to her "Everyone, this is Katie your new sister. She has learned our language pretty well, so please make her feel welcomed." Mother Jordan gave me a hug then turned me around to see the smiling faces looking at me. "Now come along, give her a hug, and let's show her how we celebrate this day."

Before she could finish, Phoebe ran over and gave me a hug and handed me pieces of cloth, the other handed me dishes for the table. Phoebe pushed me toward the table, which had grown since yesterday. Now there were two tables. The men had brought the table from outside inside to hold all the food.

Phoebe helped me set the plates on the table, and then showed me how to fold the pieces of cloth she had handed me, and place one at each plate. She said it was a napkin to wipe your fingers on after you ate. She turned to Mother Jordan and added. "I saw this displayed in one of the stores in Dubuque, and I thought I'd like to make these beautiful napkins for this year's harvest celebration. It's quite the custom back east. You place them on your lap while you're eating and then wipe your hands and mouth on them after you are finished."

I held one up to take a better look. Designs of leaves had been woven into the cloth.

Mother Jordan took one of the napkins. "Well, now, today we won't have to share the kitchen towel to wipe our hands."

Everyone laughed.

After dinner, the men went outside while the women cleaned the dishes. There wasn't much food left, but what was, stayed on the table in case anyone got hungry later. After a short time, the men came back in and added more wood to the fire. The night air grew colder, and it spoke of more snow. Everyone sat wherever they could find a spot and huddled under blankets.

Amanda turned to me. "Christmas is only a month away from now. We give presents like the present God gave us with the birth of His Son. How do you celebrate Christmas, Katie?"

I must have looked confused.

She continued. "We celebrate Christmas every year, and it's time to make plans." Amanda brushed Elsie's hair back from her face and added. "We give the presents to each other."

"What are presents?" I asked.

Father Jordan had been talking to the men but must have heard what I said because he answered. "Katie, a present is something of value you give to another person. It could be something of yours or something you make." He leaned down and picked up his boots. "I value these boots, but because I love Andrew, I want to give him a gift. Do you understand?"

"But, Father Jordan, if you give Andrew your boots, what are you going to wear?"

Everyone laughed. "No Katie, what I'm trying to say is that you give something you cherish to a loved one. What is the most precious object you have? Or better still, what would you like to give Mother Jordan? Maybe something like Phoebe made the napkins, or something else you made."

I thought for a minute. "Well, I think what I cherish most is my mother's comb. Is that what you are talking about?"

He smiled. "Yes, Katie, that's what I'm talking about. You cherish that comb because that is all you have left of your mother."

"Oh."

Even though Father Jordan explained what a gift was, I didn't think I wanted to give my mother's comb away. I didn't love anyone that much. But he didn't tell me about how his father gave his son. *I still have a lot to learn about the white man's ways.*

While I was helping Amanda put away the last of the dishes that evening, Hayden, Phoebe's husband, came to me and said. "Katie, you have made my father-in-law very happy lately. I see it in his eyes when he talks to you. I want to thank you." His smile was warm and I felt like I had known him for a long time.

"Father Jordan has been a very good friend." I laid my dishtowel down on the table. "And Mother Jordan has shown me how to do many things. Things I will need to know when I am married."

"They both love you like their own daughter. For that, I am grateful as I live very far away and only come to see them once a year for a visit." He had his hands behind his back and shifted his weight from one foot to the other. "Katie, I would like to give you a gift now. Mother told me that you are not used to wearing shoes yet and have gone barefoot. Please take this deer hide, so you can make moccasins to keep your feet warm and dry."

"I cannot do that, Hayden. I don't have anything for you."

He sat down on the chair and motioned for me to sit also. Everyone else had cleared the room. *Did they go to their beds already?* "Katie, if you would take this hide, it would make me very happy. I want to do this, because you have made my mother and father happy, especially since Samuel passed away. Please take it. You owe me nothing." He placed the hide in my hands and stood up. "Please."

I took it from him and nodded. He headed for the door to meet the men in the barn for the night. He opened the door, turned to me, and winked. "Thank you."

My own deer hide. I brought it up to my face and felt the soft hide. Hayden had already smoothed it and made it ready to sew.

Lying in bed that night my mind wandered, first

thinking of my mother and the last pair of moccasins she made for me. She carefully placed pretty beads across the top; her smile warmed me when she placed them on my feet. Even though she had hewn them, they were not as soft as the hide Hayden had given me tonight. He must have worked very hard to make them as soft as they were.

Chapter 20

November 1834

I learned much during the year following Samuel's death. The white man's harvest was a lot like my people's harvest. The women dried the seeds, put them in sacks, and buried them until our return from hunting buffalo. Upon our return, the women dug the sacks up and replanted them for a new crop. Father Jordan dried the seeds from his crop like we did, but he put them in bags that the animal feed came in, and left them in the barn during the winter.

Mother Jordan said I was getting good at drying meats and vegetables. "Katie, dear, Papa loves your sweet jam."

"I like making his favorite jam. Thank you, Mother Jordan, for showing me how to cook in your big black pot."

When we finished making the jam, we poured it into glass jars. Mother Jordan showed me how to put a small amount of candle wax on the top of the jam to seal it. "It will be good for several months with the wax," she said, "sometimes as long as a year."

I had never had sweet jam until Father Jordan showed me how to spread it on homemade bread. His favorite was strawberry jam.

Their homemade bread was something like our bread

but fixed differently. "Mother Jordan, why do you put the dough in a pan and place it in the fireplace to bake? My mother patted the dough out and laid it on a rock over wood to bake." I rubbed my stomach. "I think I like it your way a lot better."

Mother Jordan smiled. "I make bread like my mother taught me, Katie." She rubbed her hands on her white dress. "With all the things you've learned in such a short time, you'll be able to take care of your own family when you get married."

"That will be many moons from now!"

. . .

Mother Jordan showed me how to use a pattern on the deer hide Hayden gave me. "Here Katie, we've cut the moccasins, now together we can lace them up along the sides."

She took the two pieces of hide and lace and began weaving the lace in and out of the holes she had made. When that was finished, she handed me the rest of the lace and I weaved it through the holes on the top to make the fringe. Mother Jordan said I could put the beads on them when there was enough money to go into town to buy them. I looked forward to that day.

. . .

My heart still ached for my mother and father. Sometimes, even though I tried hard, I couldn't remember their faces. I felt a part of my life was gone, never to be found again, like when I lost my first pouch Mother made for me. My mother had sewn red, blue, and green beads onto it. I remember sitting and opening the flap to my pretty pouch so many times to look inside. My mother had placed a bear tooth in it. She said it would bring good spirits to watch over me. Then, when I lost the pouch, I knew I would have bad spirits watching every move I made. No matter how hard my mother tried to comfort me, she finally gave up and told my father to speak to me. She walked away, arms waving in the air, shouting, "She is your child. You talk to her."

My father took my hand and we walked away from our lodge. I cried softly. I knew my father would take care of the spirits for me. He always did. We walked for a while, not saying anything, until we reached the small stream near our lodge. He found a large rock and sat down. I sat beside him, head bowed.

"My child, sometimes our heart breaks when we lose something we hold dear to us. The pouch your mother made for you was your first, so that made it even more special in your eyes." He lifted my head to look at him. "These are things; things you can touch, see, feel. You will have more things. Many things as you get older. Your mother will make another pouch for you."

I lowered my head and cried. "But, Father, the bear's tooth was in it."

"Memekeha, look at me." He cupped my face. "These words I have spoken to you are true. The pouch and tooth are things. What you hold in your heart is what will be with you always. Have I not told you the Great Spirit is with you, always? That is what you must remember, not things of the world."

"Yes, Father, but what about the bad spirits? Mother says I should keep the bear's tooth for the good spirits."

He kissed my nose and smiled. "I will tell you again.

The bear's tooth is just an object. Would I not speak the truth? Now dry your tears and run along."

I remembered walking back to our lodge with father close behind, but his words confused me. Why would mother tell me such things about the bear's tooth if they were not true? However, when my father talked to me, he made all things better. He was a wise man and spoke wisdom. I felt safe when I was with him, and I knew nothing could ever happen to me.

This was only one of many memories, memories that were slowly fading. Somehow, try as hard as I could, other memories wouldn't appear. I wanted to remember the times my mother got so angry with me, she would walk away shaking her head and muttering to herself. I wondered why Father and Mother Jordan didn't act like that.

At night sometimes, after everyone had gone to sleep, I'd lay awake wanting to close my eyes to see my father's face. I wanted to reach out and feel the warmth of his skin, and run my finger along the scar on his cheek. He earned that scar from his encounter with a Sioux brave. My father was a fearless warrior.

Even though my mother and I didn't agree on much, she taught me how to weave baskets from the reeds along the shore of the mighty river. And how to make beads and then weave them into our clothing. Sometimes we found shells along the river's edge and mother would carefully make a hole in one end so she could string it onto her clothing. I remember thinking then how fine she looked and wondered if I would look like her when I grew up.

• • •

Many moons passed; I noticed Father Jordan seemed to

tire easily. One day, I helped him bring two big buckets of late string beans up to the cabin, so Mother Jordan could dry them like she did the rest of the vegetables.

"This will take us through the winter months," she said. "I can even make a big pot of beans and ham for dinner tonight. There's the ham bone left over from our last ham dinner three nights ago."

Father Jordan nodded his head and grinned. "That's right, Momma, don't let anything go to waste." He put his arm around her shoulder and gave her a squeeze. Mother Jordan giggled and lowered her head as if to say, "Not around the children, Papa."

Only Phoebe and her husband came that year for harvest. Even though the older, married children didn't live too far away, they weren't able to spend harvest and Christmas like last year. Mother and Father Jordan were delighted when Phoebe and family were able to make the trip. Since the death of their beloved Samuel, Father Jordan's hair started to turn white. More lines appeared on his thin face.

With Phoebe's children running around, it was nearly impossible to have a free moment with Father Jordan. I missed our quiet chats about nothing in particular or just sitting and not saying anything. Being alone with Father Jordan felt almost like being with my own father.

After the evening meal of beans, ham, and cornbread, we huddled by the blazing fireplace. The warmth of the fire covered me as I listened to stories of Father Jordan growing up in a place called North Carolina then moving here along the river. My eyes started to droop, and I found it difficult to keep them open.

Father Jordan stretched his arms over his head. "It's only two more weeks until Christmas. Everyone will be leaving to go back to their own home to settle in for the winter." He rubbed his eyes as if he might be wiping away a tear.

Phoebe's husband, Hayden, stood up abruptly. "Before we retire, we wanted to give Katie this gift we brought. It's from all of us." He handed me a large deer hide that Phoebe had been sitting on. "This is from my last hunting trip to stock up on our winter meat supply. Father Jordan said you might want to make yourself another pair of moccasins, since your moccasins from last year seem to be wearing a bit thin. Your feet may get too cold to continue using them."

I ran my fingers over it and then held it up to my face, smelling the musky scent of deer. The hide felt warm and soft. "This is so pretty, Hayden. And it's white. I always wanted a pair of white moccasins like Mother's. But, I thought you gave gifts for Christmas."

Mother Jordan leaned forward in her rocker. "My dear child, Hayden thought you might like to have this so you could make your moccasins now. That is, if that's what you want to do with the hide. It'll be getting colder closer to Christmas."

I ran my fingers over the soft hide again. "Oh, thank you. I will, I will." I ran to Hayden and threw my arms around his neck. "Thank you."

Hayden gave me a hug and turned to Phoebe. "You need to thank Phoebe, too. She helped with the tanning so it would be nice and white."

With the hide still in my hands, I walked over to Phoebe and put my arms around her neck. "Thank you Phoebe. My heart is very warm with all of your kindness."

"Nonsense my child, you're family now." Phoebe pushed

my hair back away from my face. "We want to share what we have with you."

Mother Jordan rocked and looked at me. "I know we never got the beads for you last year, but maybe later this year we can afford to buy you some."

. . .

Every day Mother and Father Jordan made me feel more like one of their own children. Father Jordan took me fishing and showed me how to weave the ropes to make a halter for the cows. Mother Jordan showed me how to sew buttons on my dress and take care of cuts and scrapes Elsie and I got when we hurt ourselves, of course, doing things we weren't supposed to do. They showed no favoritism.

In just a short time, I had shared the deepest sorrow that a person could share with a family, and then turned around to rejoice in the homecoming of their children and grandchildren. I went to bed that night feeling warm all over from the friendship and goodness of everyone. Everyone, that is, except Amanda.

The next afternoon Phoebe and Mother Jordan helped me cut out my moccasins from the deer hide. Mother Jordan held the pieces up. "My, my Katie, it looks like your feet have grown quite a bit. Maybe that was why you could see your toes peeking out of the old ones."

Phoebe and I laughed. Phoebe held up an extra piece of hide. "Look, Katie, you have a small piece left over. It's not very big but maybe you can make something else."

When I looked at it, I knew right away what it would be. "Oh yes, Phoebe, I know what to do with it." *Father Jordan could use a new pouch for his pipe tobacco.*

Mother Jordan smiled. "Would you care to share your

idea? Or do you wish to keep it to yourself?"

"I think I'd like to keep it to myself. I'll tell you later."

By the time I went to bed that night, my new moccasins were almost finished. All I had to do was to cut the fringe around the top. These were going to be prettier than the last pair, and they came almost to my knees. My legs would stay a lot warmer this winter than they did last.

I cut out Father Jordan's pouch before I went to bed. Of course, I had to cut the lace yet, but that wouldn't take very long. I imagined his excitement when I gave it to him at Christmas. Everyone was in bed when I slipped in beside Amanda. I tossed and turned most of the night, eager for the next day to come.

Two days later, Father Jordan took sick and had to go to bed. Mother Jordan said it was the fever. She and Phoebe bustled around the cabin keeping a large kettle of water boiling on the fire. A silence, like I had never experienced, hung over the family. No one said anything. All I wanted to do was sit in the chair and stare at Father Jordan's closed door.

Snow fell during the night and began sticking on the ground. When the boys went to the barn to feed the animals, they left footprints going and coming. As Hayden stepped inside, the white specks clung to his hat and shoulders. He brushed them off and hung his coat on the back of the chair. "Phoebe, how's he doing? Any change?"

"No, and I can see the worry in Mother's eyes." She wrung her hands. "Maybe we should send for the doctor from over in Dunleigh. Do you think one of the boys could go?"

No one called for the doctor unless... "Phoebe, can I see Father Jordan? Please?"

She glanced at me and back to Hayden. I could tell by

the look on her face she knew Father Jordan was very sick. "Katie, I'm not sure. Let me go in and talk to Mother first. I know you and everyone else want to talk to him. But he's very restless and burning up."

Hayden stood up and motioned for Andrew. "Come on Andrew. We're going to town to fetch the doc. The sooner the better. Go hitch up the mule."

Andrew grabbed his coat and flew out the door. He didn't have to be told the second time. Hayden put his coat back on and gave Phoebe a kiss on the cheek. "We'll be back soon."

Amanda, Elsie and I sat quietly waiting. "Phoebe, how could Father get sick so quick?" Amanda asked. "He was all right yesterday, wasn't he?"

Phoebe walked over to Amanda, licked her finger, and wiped a smudge of dirt from Amanda's cheek. "Sometimes things like this happen. We don't know the reason. I'm sure he'll be all right after the doctor takes a look at him. Why don't you bring out one of your books and read to Elsie and Katie."

Amanda looked at me and lowered her head. A tear rolled down her face. She got up and went to the shelf where Mother Jordan had a couple of books. On her way back to the table, she took Elsie's hand and led her to the chair beside her. I followed. Amanda had picked up the reading book I'd seen her look at before. She said it was the family Bible, and it had been in the Jordan family for as long as she could remember. It was worn on the edges, discolored, and some of the pages were starting to tear. Amanda began, "And when He had called His twelve disciples to Him, He gave them power over unclean spirits, to cast them out, and to heal all kinds of sickness."

Hours passed as I listened to Amanda read. I didn't understand what the words meant, but everyone else in the room seemed to hold onto each word she spoke. Almost like they felt comfort in the information. While Amanda spoke, I noticed some of the words sounded like our medicine man. *I'll have to ask Father Jordan what the words mean when he's feeling better.*

Elsie laid her head on the table and went to sleep. My wandering mind flew from my new moccasins to Father Jordan's pouch I was making him to my family, and then back to anticipating Hayden and Andrew's return with the doctor. Mother Jordan and Phoebe busied themselves preparing food for the evening meal. They took turns going into the sleeping room to check on Father Jordan. Neither said anything, just shook their heads and closed his door.

We heard hoofs pounding then coming to a stop. The door flew open and Hayden stepped inside removing his gloves. "The doc is right behind us. Andrew's putting the mule in the barn and will feed the animals before he comes in." He kissed Phoebe on the forehead and sat down. "Doc says there's quite a few in town not feeling well right now. Same condition--bad fever and chills."

Phoebe handed him a cup of hot coffee and pushed a stray piece of hair that had fallen into her face back behind her ear. "Momma is really worried. It's not like Father to get sick. He's always the one to take care of the family."

Mother Jordan closed the door to the sleeping room behind her. "I heard what you said, Hayden. We need to pray Papa will get well soon." She walked over to the fireplace, poured herself a cup of coffee, and sat down beside Hayden. "How far behind you is the doctor?"

Hayden stroked her hand. "He should be here real soon,

Momma. He was hitching his horse to the wagon when we left."

As Andrew came through the door, we saw the doctor pull up to the porch. He threw the reins over the post, and took two large steps into the house and placed his bag on the table. "Hello Mrs. Jordan, Phoebe. Is Mr. Jordan in the other room?"

Mother Jordan stood up. "Doctor, can I get you something to drink first?"

"No, Mrs. Jordan, let me take a look at him first. Then I'll take a cup of hot coffee. There's a pretty good chill in the air." He rubbed his hands together, laid his jacket on the back of the chair, and picked up his bag from the table.

Mother Jordan led him to the sleeping room. The lump in my throat felt as big as the watermelon in Mother Jordan's garden. I thought I would never be able to swallow ever again. Amanda closed the Bible, but her finger marked the page where she stopped reading.

"Phoebe, do you want me to take Elsie in and put her to bed?" I thought if I did something, it would take my mind off the doctor and Father Jordan. I needed to do anything other than sitting here looking at each other.

Phoebe looked at me, but I wasn't sure if she was really looking at me. "Huh?" She looked at Elsie. "Oh, yes, please, would you do that, Katie? She is just tuckered out. I'd like you to do that."

Eager to keep busy, I walked over to Elsie and nudged her arm. She looked up at me with her eyes half open. "Come on, Elsie. Let me get you to bed so you can rest better."

She stood up, looked around at everyone, and then followed me to her sleeping box. I helped her cover up and kissed her on the forehead. With half-closed eyes, she asked, "Is Papa going to be all right?"

I sat down beside her and rubbed her back. "I'm sure of it, Elsie." I waited until she fell asleep and she was breathing deep before I went back to where everyone else sat waiting for the doctor to emerge. Hayden sipped his coffee, Phoebe continued to pace the floor, Amanda read the Bible quietly to herself, and Andrew sat at the table with his face in his hands.

Darkness fell outside. I'm not sure how long we waited, but it seemed like hours before the door opened and the doctor walked out. Mother Jordan followed. "Mrs. Jordan, he's going to need a lot of rest. It's the same thing as the others have in town, just a very bad case of influenza. He should show some signs of improvement in a few days."

Mother Jordan walked over to the stove and picked up a cup. "Have a seat Doc, and warm up. Let me fix you something to eat. It's dark outside and quite late. Won't you think about staying the night then head back to town in the morning?"

He took the coffee and sat down. "That's mighty tempting, but I probably should be heading back. With so many others sick, they may need me."

Phoebe handed him a plate of left over ham and green beans. "I do wish you'd reconsider."

"Thank you for the offer, but I'd better get back. Like I said, Mr. Jordan should be as good as new in a week with plenty of rest. If you need me, send someone into town, and I'll be back out as quickly as I can."

As soon as the doctor finished cleaning his plate, he stood up. "I really must be going. Thanks again for that hot plate of food. Not often I get ham and beans plus the cornbread."

Chapter 21

November 1834

Deep racking sobs woke me three days later. Was I dreaming? I lay in bed with my blanket pulled up to my chin staring at the ceiling, listening. There it was again. I rolled over, swung my feet over the side of the bed, and walked to the door. From the slight opening, I noticed Phoebe embracing Amanda. They both wept. Phoebe wiped her eyes with her apron. My stomach fell to my feet, leaving a hole where it should have been.

I could barely get the words out. My mouth felt as dry as the seeds I helped Father Jordan plant last spring. "What's wrong?"

My head turned toward the sleeping room as the door swung open. Mother Jordan stood in the doorway as white as the new snow on the ground. I knew before she said it. "Papa has gone on to meet his Maker. He is at peace."

Amanda and I rushed into her open arms, and buried our faces in her apron. Her fragrance filled my nostrils.

I don't know how long we stood there entwined, each in our own thoughts, softly whimpering. *This can't be happening. We were going to cut a tree to decorate; I need to finish my gift for Father Jordan; there's the spring planting.*

I knew if I just sat down for a while, Father Jordan would come through the door. *Please, Father Jordan...*

Phoebe interrupted my thoughts. "Mama, we have a lot to do. I'll fix something to eat for everyone." She turned toward the table and with one hand lifted the empty pot to fill with water while brushing tears from her eyes. "Andrew is out feeding the animals with Hayden. I need to fix some coffee to warm them."

From my spot on the floor, I watched as Amanda set the table. Mother Jordan went back into the sleeping room. We were going about our everyday chores as if we were in a trance.

Elsie came to me rubbing the sleep from her eyes. "Why is everyone crying, Katie?"

How could I tell her that her Papa was dead? She lost her big brother last year and now this. I pulled her closer and she sat down next to me, almost on my lap. "Elsie, Father Jordan has passed on. I'm so sorry." I held her close. My family was gone, and now I was enduring the same loss with my new family.

She smiled at me. Oh, that's all right, Katie. Now he can talk to Samuel. I'll miss him, but he really missed Samuel."

I didn't know what to say. The door flew open and Hayden stepped inside saving me an answer.

He took his coat off and put his arms around Phoebe. "What's wrong? Is Papa all right?"

New tears welled in Phoebe's eyes as she turned around to face her husband. "No, Hayden, Papa passed on a few minutes ago. Someone needs to go into town and let the doctor know."

Hayden paused, swallowed hard, and his face turned gray. I knew he was close to Father Jordan, but from the look on his face, it was as if he lost more than his father-in-law. "I'll ride in as soon as I get a bite to eat. How's Mama?" His body fell into the chair.

Phoebe brushed away a tear. "I think she knew his time was near but didn't want any of us to know it. Mama is a strong woman."

Why is everyone so quiet, almost like Father Jordan had never been here? Everyone spoke in hushed tones, half-conscious of what was going on around them. My mother would be wailing, loud, and pulling her long hair, along with the other women in the village. Our men would be playing drums and chanting. I felt sure I would never get used to the white man's ways.

. . .

I don't know how I got through the next two days. Phoebe and Mother Jordan busied themselves preparing food for visitors that dropped by. Mother Jordan dressed Father Jordan in his best suit. He lay in their bed for people to come in and say goodbye.

Mother Jordan barely spoke. I watched in wonder as she went through the motions from morning to evening. She embraced visitors, helped Phoebe prepare meals, and still made sure each of us looked our best the day the preacher showed up. A few of Father Jordan's friends came the second day to help dig the grave, his final resting place.

"At least he will be close to us," Mother Jordan said. "and I can go talk to him whenever I want."

Even though the ground was hard, the men were able to dig down a few feet. "They'll have to dig a deeper grave when the thaw comes," Hayden said.

When the time came, dark clouds hung overhead and

the cold clung to my body even with the long underwear Mother Jordan said I needed to wear. My moccasins were warm and hugged my legs all the way to my knees. Hayden said the men hoped it wouldn't snow before they laid Father Jordan in the ground. Maybe that was what we needed; snow, to cover the darkness of our surroundings.

I fell into step behind Amanda and Elsie as we walked the short distance to the family cemetery. My mind wandered back to another time I followed them when they buried Samuel. *Great Spirit,* I prayed, *you have taken my family, and now you are taking my new family one at a time. I do not know why I have angered you. Have I been a bad person?*

The preacher cleared his throat. "We gather here today to say goodbye to our friend, Thomas Jordan, a fine, upright, honest man who loved his family. A friend to everyone he met. Let us sing a song of praise."

The family and friends sang a song I'd heard before in Father Jordan's church. I still didn't know the words but I tried to hum as they sang *Rock of Ages*. Mother Jordan's voice sounded muffled when she sang. She dabbed her eyes with her handkerchief from time to time while she held Elsie's hand.

The preacher continued and the people sang more songs until I saw Mother Jordan go forward and throw dirt on top of the container that held Father Jordan's body. Andrew told me it was his casket.

Inching my way forward until I stood beside Mother Jordan, I reached into my pocket and pulled out the tobacco pouch. I had been so excited that I had something beautiful to give Father Jordan that Christmas. The soft deerskin felt smooth between my fingers. I dropped to my knees and threw the pouch onto the box. More dirt followed and soon covered his casket. Too weary to move, I sat down and stared at the mound of dirt. Hayden hammered a cross into the ground with Father Jordan's name on it. He had etched letters and numbers on the wood: *Thomas Jordan 1768-1834.*

Mother Jordan's hand on my shoulder startled me. "Come along, Katie. It's getting colder; I don't want you to catch your death sitting on that cold ground. Papa wouldn't want you to get sick either."

I didn't want to leave Father Jordan yet. "Mother Jordan, can I stay just for a little bit? I won't get cold."

"Katie, much to my dismay, I think you need to come in, but if you promise me you will only stay for a few minutes, then I'll let you stay." She bent over to look directly into my eyes. "I have a question. You don't have to tell me, but why did you throw the pouch on Papa's casket?"

I looked into her tired but beautiful eyes. "He has to have it when he travels to his new home. I made it for him to keep his tobacco dry. My people always leave things for our dead to travel with, so they will be prepared when they reach their new home."

We were both silent for a moment. "Oh, Katie," Mother Jordan said, "that was very thoughtful of you. I'm sure Papa will appreciate it. Now remember, don't stay here too long. I'll have something hot for you to drink when you get to the cabin." She squeezed my shoulder, turned around and headed back to the cabin. The others had gone on before her.

...

It was quiet, so very quiet. I didn't feel the cold so much now. I spoke aloud to Father's grace. "Father Jordan, why did you have to leave me, too? We were going to go fishing again next summer. You even fixed a pole of my very own."

Something cold hit my nose. I looked up and saw white flecks floating down, a few at a time. I stuck out my tongue as one landed on it—cold and wet. Tears slid down my face. Now I knew why my mother wailed so loudly when we buried our dead. I wanted to do that now. I pulled my legs up, wound my arms around them, and rocked back and forth. Hot wet tears streamed down my face. *Why, Great Spirit, why do you take family away from me?*

Chapter 22

Dubuque, Iowa 1916

Grandma played with my hair as we rocked. She sat silent for a long time. I wanted to hear more. Even though I'd heard the story before, I never got tired of hearing it. "Grandma, tell me what happened next. How long did you sit on the cold ground at Father Jordan's grave?"

She smiled her warm smile. "My little butterfly, I don't remember how long I sat at his grave, but I know that hot cup of cocoa sure warmed me up when I finally got to the cabin."

"Grandma, how long did you stay with the Jordan family? What happened to Mother Jordan? And Amanda? Why didn't all Father Jordan's family come for his funeral? And..."

"Hold on, my child. You are full of questions for such a little butterfly." She laughed. "It seems like so long ago now."

Grandma got that faraway look again. "Grandma, when did you meet Grandpa? How did you meet him?"

"I guess you're not going to be quiet until I finish my story, are you?"

"No, I want to hear more, please. And whatever

happened to your mother's comb you found? You know, the one you put in your pouch?"

She stopped rocking and put her hand in the pocket of her apron. "You mean this one?"

She held it up so I could see it better. It was yellowed by time, but I could see the carving on it. "Can I hold it?"

"My little butterfly, this will be yours when I am no longer here. When you hold it, remember the stories I have told you. Think of the love my father had for my mother when he carved this out of bone for her."

I ran my fingers across the teeth of the comb and traced the carving along the top. "What do the marks mean? What was your mother's name?"

Her fingers slowly traced along the markings. "Her name was Kat-e-quah. I wish I could remember what the markings are, but sadly, I do not. It was so long ago."

With that, she put the comb back into her pocket, and leaned back in the rocker and began rocking again.

"Grandma, are you going to finish the story? Why didn't all the children come for the funeral? Are you going to tell me about Grandpa? And do you remember what your mother's name meant?"

"No, dear one, I wish I could remember what her name meant. I think it was something like eagle, great eagle. But, no, I don't remember with certainty. The rest of Father Jordan's children lived too far away to get home in time for his funeral. So, no, they couldn't get there in time. And, yes, my child." She nodded. "Yes, I will tell you more about my story."

I snuggled closer to Grandma as she wrapped her plump arms tightly around me. My fingers traced the wrinkles on her weathered hands.

Phoebe and Hayden stayed until Christmas the year Father Jordan died, then packed their children and wagon and headed back to Iowa. I saw tears again in Mother Jordan's eyes when they pulled out that brisk, snowy morning. Elsie and I stood next to Mother Jordan waving goodbye until we could no longer see their wagon. Amanda had stayed in the cabin. Mother Jordan said it upset her too much to see Phoebe leave. Andrew went back to the barn to finish his chores as soon as Hayden clicked the reins. I guess he didn't want to see them leave either. Hayden kissed my forehead and rumpled my hair before climbing into the wagon. "Katie, you are the best thing to happen to this family. Always remember that. Father Jordan loved you very much, and I know Mother Jordan does, too. If you ever need anything, remember, I will be here."

As I stood there watching them slowly disappear, I felt like another part of me slipping away. I didn't understand why family had to live so far apart. In our camp, families stayed together, helping each other. The women cleaned hides together, dried meat together, and taught the girls how to make clothing together. *I don't think I will get used to white man's ways.*

Mother Jordan wiped her hands on her apron. "Well, girls, let's get to work. You know there is always work to be done. Elsie, go gather the eggs. Katie, come with me and let's get the cabin in order."

I watched as Elsie quickly ran off to the chicken coop, then I turned and followed Mother Jordan into the cabin. Amanda sat at the table, head bowed, crying softly.

Mother Jordan went to her and laid her hand on her shoulder. "Amanda, the hurt will never go away, but it will get better in time. Think of it this way, you will be getting married soon and you will be leaving, too."

Amanda looked up at Mother Jordan as she wiped tears from her eyes. "I don't think it will ever get better, Mama." She stood up, brushed past me, toward the sleeping room, and closed the door.

Mother Jordan looked at me and shook her head. "It's hard on all of us, but we'll be all right. We must work together to take care of the farm." She reached over and tucked my wild strand of hair behind my ear. "And each other."

I tried to be more cheerful than I felt. "I'll help you, Mother Jordan. Tell me what you want me to do."

She smiled. "I know you will. I am very lucky to have you, Katie. Yes, very lucky indeed."

The door flew open and Elsie bounced in carrying a basket full of eggs. "Mama, look how many eggs I got. There was a lot out there." She placed the basket on the table. "Can we have scrambled eggs for supper? Please, Mama, can we?"

Mother Jordan chuckled. "Yes, Elsie, I'll fix scrambled eggs for you. I think you could eat eggs three times a day if I'd let you. Call Andrew and see if he needs help, then get washed up for supper."

Elsie and I ran out the door together to check on Andrew, and, of course, to see if he needed help with the animals.

Chapter 23

Summer 1839

The next six years flew by. Andrew had asked Mary Ann Waddell, a girl in town, to marry him, and everyone was busy making plans for the big day. Mother Jordan said the bride's parents did most of the preparations and they'd be married in the bride's home. *A wedding sure required a lot of work.* In my village, the woman getting married made a new dress with many beads and feathers. The man prepared a new wigwam for his woman. Dancing and chanting with drums took place at the ceremony. Then the couple went into their wigwam for many days.

Amanda helped Mother Jordan bake cookies for the refreshments. Elsie joined in by finishing the last embroidery stitches on the kitchen towels to give as a wedding gift, from the family. Even though we were able to do something for the couple, times were beginning to take a toll on our family. I noticed Mother Jordan had a few more lines around her mouth and forehead.

Late one evening, when Mother Jordan thought everyone was in bed, I found her reading her Bible by the oil lamp. I tiptoed closer and whispered, "Why are you up so late? You should be getting your rest like the rest of the family."

She smiled. "I find comfort reading the Good Book. It seems like this is the only time I can find to read it."

I sat down on the floor beside her. "Why do you call it the Good Book? I thought it was a Bible?"

She closed the book. "My dear child, the Bible is the good book. It's God's Word for us to live by. I know it's confusing, but when I read it, I feel comfort, I feel at peace."

Her face looked drawn, but soft. The light from the oil lamp flickered upon her face and I saw calmness. I also saw strength, her strength that held everyone else together. I wondered how she did it. Who helped her? Was it the book she held close?

I remembered going to the building they called their church with Father and Mother Jordan. Mother Jordan held her book very tight.

"But Katie, what are you doing up at this hour? You should be in bed yourself."

"Oh. I thought I heard something. Maybe it was you." I stood up. "You need sleep, like the rest of us. I'll see you in the morning." I took her hand and pulled her to her feet.

. . .

Andrew and Mary Ann's wedding day finally arrived, with the sun peeking over the tops of the trees. Andrew wore his newly pressed suit and each of us donned our best clothes. Mother Jordan sat next to Andrew as he drove the wagon three miles south to the Waddell's home. The Franklin, Green, and Smith families had already arrived.

As soon as we unloaded the wagon, Elsie, Amanda, and I followed Mother Jordan into the house. The Waddell's home was small like the Jordan's. Several women were standing around Mary Ann when we stepped inside. Mrs. Waddell stepped aside, and I saw Mary Ann standing in her beautiful dress. It was made of silk, with Irish crocheted lace at the bodice. It was ivory and had a high waist and short puffy sleeves. She wore an Irish lace cap on her head. I was proud of myself as I was beginning to learn more about fabric from Mother Jordan. She said she would teach me how to make a dress soon. Mary Ann looked pretty, and I felt Andrew had chosen wisely.

Tables lined with more food than possibly could be eaten awaited the guests in the Waddell backyard. The cookies Elsie and Mother Jordan made sat next to a pretty chocolate cake baked by Mary Ann's mother. Bowls of fried potatoes and pots of beans and ham sat on each end of the table. Right in the middle of the food sat three big bowls of fried chicken. Homemade bread filled six baskets. My mouth watered.

Farmers from miles around came to congratulate the couple. I noticed several men with funny looking instruments playing music while couples danced. I had never heard these instruments before, but the music from them reminded me of wind blowing through the trees. One man held something up to his mouth, and it sounded like taking two reeds from the riverbeds and blowing through them. Mother Jordan called it a harmonica.

I stood by one of the food tables wondered which piece of chicken I should take when two women approached. When one woman noticed me, she cupped her hand over her mouth, turned, and whispered to the woman with a big mole on her nose. They then turned their backs to me, giggling. One time, the one with the mole on her nose turned to look at me again. I felt funny, uncomfortable. I remembered the woman with the mole from Mr. Goodnight's store. She was the one that spoke sharply to Mother Jordan about me. She made me feel ill at ease even then. No longer hungry, I turned and walked away to find Mother Jordan. When I found her, I made sure I stayed by her side for the rest of the day.

A few guests danced well into the night while others slowly gathered their children and the dishes they had brought, and left. Mother Jordan said, "It's time for all of us to head home. Come along, Katie." She wrapped her arm around my shoulder. "I believe Amanda and Elsie are waiting with Andrew at the wagon. It's been a very long day and everyone must be tired."

We all loaded into the wagon along with Andrew and Mary Ann ready to head home. Mrs. Waddell stood and waved as she clutched her handkerchief and gently cried as we got ready to drive away. Mr. Waddell took hold of the bridle and told Andrew to take good care of his daughter. He slapped Ole' Jeb on his neck and let go of the reins.

Chapter 24

Spring 1850

Andrew and Mary Ann stayed with Mother Jordan for a year while he built their new home on a small piece of land he bought fifteen miles away. They packed their wagon and drove over every three days to work on it. Once, Elsie and I got to go with them. Andrew's cabin wasn't much bigger than Mother Jordan's, but he said they didn't need much space right now. He told Mother Jordan once the children started coming, they'd add more rooms. I supposed that was the way of white people—just adding more rooms as their family grew.

Soon after Andrew and Mary Ann moved out, Amanda married James Snodgrass, and six months later Elsie married James Sloan. Both Amanda and Elsie moved farther west. Only Mother Jordan and I remained to take care of the planting, milking, and repairs. I became quite handy with a hammer.

One night, after we had cleaned the table and put everything away, Mother Jordan motioned to me. "Katie, come over here and sit by me. I need to talk with you."

She sounded so tired. I couldn't imagine what she could have wanted to talk to me about. By the time we fed the few animals we had left, fixed our meal, and put away the dishes, we were tired, and usually went straight to bed. Tonight felt different. Mother Jordan headed for her rocker and sat down. She cleared her throat and motioned for me to take a seat also.

"It's only you and me now since everyone has married and left. I've thought this over and over. Katie, I'm so sorry to have to ask you this." She sighed and began again. "We may lose the farm if I don't get some money soon. You know we've had to cut back on the feed for the animals." She wrung her hands then smoothed her apron. "I've already sold most of our cows and now it looks like I'll have to sell our mule."

For the first time since I met this lovely woman, she looked tired and helpless. I knew I had to do something to help. My stomach knotted. She and Father Jordan had always been there for me, and now, I needed to be there for her. "Do you want me to find work? I can take care of you. You've taken good care of me for a long time." I knelt down beside her. "Now it's my turn to help you."

"You know I hate to ask you, but I don't know what else to do."

I thought she would cry. "That's all right. You've taught me how to clean and cook. You've taught me how to do that. Maybe I can work for someone else who will pay me." My fingers gently stroked her weathered hands. "I can give you the money, so you won't lose the farm."

Her calloused hands caressed my face. "As a matter of fact, I think I do know someone" She leaned back in her rocker. There is this lady; I think her name is Ginger. Anyway, the last time we were in town, I overhead her asking Mr. Goodnight, in the general store, if he knew of a housekeeper."

"Does she live in town, too?"

Mother Jordan sat quiet for a while, her eyes closed. I didn't know if she was thinking, or if she had fallen asleep. Lately, I noticed her nodding off every now and then while sitting in her rocker. Slowly she opened her eyes and her gaze fell upon my face. She sighed. "I think she does live in town, but I'm not sure where. And I can't imagine why she needs a housekeeper. I didn't think she was married or had children. Then again, I haven't kept up with everyone in town lately, so she could be married and have a house full of children." She covered my hands with hers. "Only one way to find out, my child. We'll go into town tomorrow. Now, off to bed for both of us. Morning comes early."

I stood up and kissed her on her soft cheek. "Good night, Mother Jordan. I'll be ready early."

Tomorrow was going to be a big day. *I've always stayed on the farm, except for a few trips into town, but if I go to work for someone in town, that will change. Some of those women in their fancy dresses still look at me differently. Like I don't belong around them. It makes me feel bad, like they think I will give them a disease if I touch them. What can I do to make them feel better around me?*

• • •

I reined the mule in and jumped down from the wagon. Mother Jordan waited patiently as I came around to help her manage the step down. As frail as her years had made her, she was still spry and tried to do everything for herself. Sometimes I had to tell her that certain chores were for me to do. "Remember, I'm younger than you, I often told her."

"I can still take care of myself, young lady," was her

usual reply.

Once inside the store, the smell of fresh coffee filled my nostrils. Mother Jordan spoke first. "That smell is heaven this morning, especially after our early morning trip."

Mr. Goodnight looked up from his paperwork. "Good Morning, Mrs. Jordan. And a good morning to you too, Katie. Could I get you both a fresh cup?" He pointed to a couple of chairs sitting close to a big barrel. "Go on over there and have a seat. What brings you two into town this early? Everything all right on the farm?"

Mother Jordan and I promptly seated ourselves, brushing our skirts, and sat back in the barrel chairs. "Oh, my goodness, Mr. Goodnight, everything is fine on the farm. But, we do have business here in town."

Mr. Goodnight brought two steaming cups of coffee and handed them to us. I cradled the cup with both hands, letting the liquid warm me. As I brought it to my lips, I watched Mother Jordan through the steam. I hadn't realized how much I missed my coffee in the morning until I took my first sip. The toasty liquid ran down my throat and chest landing like a thud in the pit of my empty stomach. I'd been making the coffee ever since Father Jordan passed away. It was nice to have a cup that someone else made. *I think I will drink it slow and savor it.* I'd been in such a hurry to get to town; I forgot to eat the biscuit Mother Jordan had fixed for me.

Mr. Goodnight walked back to the counter and began to straighten bolts of cloth. He turned when Mother Jordan began. "Mr. Goodnight, I overheard the woman, Ginger, say she was looking for a housekeeper. Do you know if she's found one?"

He smoothed his hand over the cloth. It looked like he

was thinking—of what, I couldn't tell. "Well, Mrs. Jordan, as far as I know she has not found anyone. I can send Matthew over to her place and see if she's available to come over and talk to you. Would that be all right?"

"Oh, yes, Mr. Goodnight, that would be lovely." She looked down at her hands and back to Mr. Goodnight. She cleared her throat, like she was trying to take her time to answer. "That is, if it isn't an imposition."

I knew asking Mr. Goodnight for information was hard on Mother Jordan but asking me to go to work and help out was even harder. I felt bad for her, and tried to reassure her I would do anything to help. She had become my mother, my friend, and my confidant. Since the death of Father Jordan and Samuel, I felt her closeness even more. Then when everyone left, she clung to me even more. Mr. Goodnight startled my thoughts.

"Nonsense, it's no imposition. Both of you just sit right here and keep me company while Matthew runs over to see if she is able to come to the store. Besides, I haven't seen you or talked to you in a long time. We have some things to get caught up on."

Mother Jordan blushed.

Between the "did you know so and so was visiting her sister out of town" and "can you believe he was caught drinking in the saloon when he was supposed to be helping Mr. Campbell with his new mare," and another cup of coffee followed by a plate of sugar cookies, it seemed like an hour before Ginger walked through the door behind Matthew.

The smallest woman I had ever seen stepped inside the door. Her hat looked almost bigger than she did. Approaching Mother Jordan, she held out her hand. She spoke in an accent I had never heard before. "Good morning, ma'am, my name is Ginger."

Mother Jordan stood up and shook hands. "Good morning, Ginger. My name is Mrs. Jordan and this is my daughter, Katie." She turned to me.

Her green eyes sparkled when she spoke. "Well good morning, Katie." She turned to Mother Jordan again. "And what do I owe the pleasure of this visit?"

Mr. Goodnight pulled another chair up and we all sat. Mother Jordan began. "I heard that you may be looking for help in your home. Is that true?"

Ginger looked over at me then back to Mother Jordan. She smoothed her beautiful skirts and removed her gloves. Not many women wore gloves around town. "Mrs. Jordan, yes, indeed, I am looking for someone to help me keep my home in shape." She turned to me. "How old are you child? You don't look like you could be sixteen yet."

I looked at Mother Jordan then back at Ginger. "I am eighteen and I can do whatever you need me to do." My hands were sweating.

"She's a good worker," Mother Jordan chimed in. "She's as strong as any man. I have taught her to cook and clean. We wouldn't be asking, but we could use the money." Mother Jordan hung her head, and I saw a tear slip down her cheek.

I got up and went to her, put my arms around her. "Please, Miss Ginger, I can do the work you need done."

Ginger stood up. "Do you live nearby?"

"About three miles out."

"Well, come along, child. Let me show you the work I would need you to do. Mrs. Jordan, please come too. I'd like you to see what your daughter will be doing for her keep and wages." She turned, put on her gloves, and proceeded out the door.

Mother Jordan and I just looked at each other. "Does that mean I have a job?"

We followed Ginger and fell in step with her. Not a word was spoken as our skirts dragged the dusty street and passed the saloon then the millinery. Ginger turned when we approached a neat house sitting behind a small picket fence. "Well, here it is, ladies."

I thought she said she lived just outside of town so I was surprised on how quickly we arrived. Her house sat probably not quite a quarter mile past the livery stable. That was the best I could tell anyway. You could still see Main Street from her front porch. Close enough to walk to town but far enough so you don't hear all the noises. "You don't live in town, do you?"

"No, my dear, I prefer the quiet life, away from all the noise. Come inside and see what you'll be doing." We followed her through the gate and up one step on the rough wooden porch lined with beautiful flowers.

I tugged on Mother Jordan's arm. "Mother Jordan what are those flowers called? I've never seen anything so pretty."

"I'm not quite sure. I don't think I've seen flowers like those before either."

Ginger opened the door. "Oh, those are Daylilies. I had them sent in from Chicago. Beautiful, aren't they? Ladies, come in." She held the door for us. I gasped.

"So pretty, "Mother Jordan and I said in unison.

I was curious. "Are you from Chicago? I was just wondering, since your flowers are from Chicago."

"Please, come over here and take a seat." She laid her dainty purse on the table. "Land sakes no, but I've visited, and I did fall in love with the Daylilies. I'm from the

Carolinas."

No sooner had we sat down at the table when a woman came in from another room. "Miss Ginger, may I get something for you to drink?"

"Yes, please. Mrs. Jordan, may I get you some tea? Coffee? Katie, will you have something, too? This is Delia, my companion."

I wasn't sure what she meant when she said companion. It looked like she was a maid and I wondered why she needed another person to help clean this small house. I extended my hand toward Delia. "My name is Katie." We shook hands.

Ginger took off her gloves and sat down across from Mother Jordan and me. The yellow flowers on the table came to her chin, highlighting her long red hair. Not many women wore their hair down. Most of them tied their hair back and pinned it on top of their head like Mother Jordan did. That kept it out of the way when taking care of chores all day. Something was different about this woman.

Mother Jordan broke the silence. "Could we get down to business? I'd like to know what my daughter will be doing for you. You have a companion helping you right now. Is she leaving?"

Ginger laughed lightly. "Oh, no, Delia has been my companion for many years. She takes care of me, has taken care of me since I was twelve. But that's another story."

Delia returned and set a tray with a teapot, cups, and saucers in front of Ginger. I looked around the vase of flowers and saw another plate filled with cookies. Ginger filled each cup with hot liquid and passed it to each of us. Then she handed Mother Jordan a napkin and the plate of cookies. "Please, have one of these delicious treats. Delia is an excellent cook. Sometimes I wonder why I haven't busted my corset with all of her wonderful cooking." She gave a robust laugh.

Again, I wondered why Ginger wanted someone else to help her.

We settled in our chairs sipping our tea. Ginger began. "I know you're wondering why I need someone here to assist me. As you see, I have Delia, but she will be going to my place of business to help there. I need someone here to keep my house clean, to cook my meals, and cook meals for my girls. Do you think you can do that?"

Miss Ginger didn't say she had a place of business. "I know I can do that for you. Don't you think so, Mother Jordan?" I looked at her pleading.

"Well, my child, as much as I hate for you to go to work, I know you can do what Miss Ginger is asking of you." She set her cup down and placed her hands on her lap. She began wringing them, like she did when she was nervous. "If you don't mind me asking but what does Delia do in your business and what will my daughter's wages be?"

"Oh my," Ginger giggled. "My wonderful Delia takes care of my books—she is much better with numbers than I am. And about your wages, well, now, how does room and board plus two dollars a month sound to you both?" She fanned herself with her handkerchief. "And, of course, Katie will stay here for five days and go home for two. That way she can help you and me at the same time. Does that sound like something you can work with?"

We looked at each other then back to Ginger. "Mother Jordan?" I said.

"Yes, Ginger." Mother Jordan said. "We can work with that schedule. Thank you. Oh, I almost forgot. You said you have girls working for you—what do they do? And, when does Katie start work?"

"Well, yes. I should have told you what they do, not wait for you to ask." She cleared her throat and dabbed her forehead with her hanky. "The four girls help around my shop, but none of them know how to cook. That's the main reason I need your daughter's help. Delia's been cooking, but she can't do the books and cook, too."

I looked at Mother Jordan and back to Ginger. We said in unison. "Oh."

"Was that it?"

"Yes, I was just curious," Mother Jordan said.

"Good, then it's settled. Katie, you're my new employee." She shook my hand again.

Ginger stood up. "Come along, Katie. Let me show you where you'll be staying. You, too, Mrs. Jordan. I want you to see also. That way you will feel more at ease knowing she'll be taken good care of." We followed her into the kitchen. "Delia is more familiar with the kitchen so she will show you where everything is." We followed her to a room just off the kitchen. It was small, but it had a bed, dresser and chair.

"This is so pretty, Ginger." I ran my hand over the dresser.

"That was made by Delia's father. I've had it for a long time. Come along; let me show you the rest of the house."

We followed her back through the kitchen and to the main room where we originally sat and had tea. Then we proceeded into a small hall with two doors just. The first room had lacy curtains on the window, a spread on the bed to match the curtains, and pretty cloth napkins on the dresser. "Ladies, this is my room. I guess you could tell that when you stepped in. Now, let me show you where Delia sleeps." Four steps down the hall, we entered another room. This one was much like the room off the kitchen, only bigger. I noticed another dresser just like the one in my quarters. Ginger noticed me staring at it. "When Delia's father made the first one, he also made another one for me. You'll be using the one he made me."

After the tour and tears, we decided I might as well begin now since I had packed a small bag if someone needed me immediately. I bid goodbye to Mother Jordan.

She assured me she could handle the wagon going home. "I've been handling this old mule and wagon long before you were even born. I'll see you in five days when I bring the wagon in and pick you up. I love you, Katie. I'm going to miss you, but I'll be fine."

"Goodbye, Mother Jordan." I wiped my eyes. "I'll miss you, too. Don't worry about me. I'll be good and you can be proud of me."

Chapter 25

Summer 1850

This was the first time I'd ever been away from Mother Jordan. By day, work kept my mind from worrying about her. At night, I'd lie awake wondering what she was doing. A couple of times, I caught myself asking the Great Spirit to watch over her. Then, to make sure she would be all right, I'd added that same prayer to Mother Jordan's Father as well. I wanted to make sure she was going to be fine without me; still, I wondered if He heard me.

I cleaned Ginger's house daily, and did laundry once a week. Ginger wasn't home much, so I spent hours wandering through the rooms looking at the few pictures she had hanging on the walls, wondering who they were, running my fingers across the pretty glass containers on her dresser. One container held toilet water, as Ginger called it. The light fragrance smelled of flowers. Once I put some behind my ears as I saw her do when she was dressed and ready to head to town. All day the smell drifted across my nose, and I thought of the pretty flowers outside the door.

Ginger didn't say much when she got home. Both she and Delia came home together in the early morning hours, tired, hungry, and ready for bed. I wondered what kind of business Ginger had to keep them out all night. Everyone I knew got up early and worked all day then went to bed early sleeping all night.

Delia came home when the sun set and picked up the meals I prepared for the working girls. Later, when she and Ginger came home in the morning, she brought the dishes with her. The meals I cooked were quite generous portions and each night the bowls were scraped clean. All of them seemed to like the special corn pudding Mother Jordan taught me how to make.

Every day Delia and Ginger ate a hardy breakfast of eggs, sausage, and biscuits close to noon. Sometimes I wished I could remember how to fix the breads my mother made. I wanted to show Ginger that I could bake bread instead of biscuits. Occasionally, I could taste Mother's bread, and my mouth watered.

One evening, Matthew showed up instead of Delia. I was surprised when I answered the door. "Hello, Matthew. What brings you out here?"

"Delia asked me to pick up the food you prepared and bring it to the girls. She was busy and couldn't come."

Matthew seemed to be an errand boy for the mercantile store and several other businesses in town. He had come here several other times. "I just finished the last touches on the meals." My mind raced ahead. *Maybe he'll tell me what kind of business Ginger operates.* "Matthew, how well do you know Ginger?"

He followed me into the kitchen. "I don't know her very well, just since she came to town about a year ago. She was the prettiest lady I'd ever seen. When she stepped down from the coach, every man on the street stopped what he was doing and stared at her. Why do you ask?"

I placed the last bowl in the basket and covered it. Matthew was still a young boy, probably not much older than I was. His dark brown hair curled around his ears and across his high forehead. "Well I was wondering what kind of business Ginger has. Do you know?"

His brown eyes deepened as a frown developed. "Oh, well, Katie, I don't know if I should be telling you. Miss Ginger should tell you." He reached for the basket.

My hand grabbed the handle. "Why can't you tell me?"

"Well, uummm, Katie, it's not that you shouldn't know, but, well…"

"What's so bad that you can't tell me? I want to know right now, Matthew." I stood my ground and placed my hands on my hips. After all, I was making food for the girls that worked for Ginger. I worked for Ginger, and I should know where they worked. I looked him square in the eyes.

He squirmed, looked at me, and then down to his feet. I saw a red flush start on his neck then spread to his face going all the way to the top of his forehead. "Katie, you might not like what I'm going to tell you. Miss Ginger has girls that entertain men at the saloon."

"What do you mean entertain? That can't be so bad."

"It means the girls sing and then the men buy the girls drinks. Are you satisfied now that you made me tell you?"

He grabbed the basket before I could stop him. "Wait, can I go with you? I want to see."

"No!" He ran out the door.

My mouth flew open. *What's so wrong with the girls singing and drinking?* I would have to ask Mother Jordan next time I see her. Maybe she could tell me why Matthew was so upset about telling me. In the back of my mind, I began thinking of how I could get to the saloon and see the girls for myself.

Ginger and Delia came home their usual time with the empty basket. I wanted to ask if I could visit the girls, but thought better of it. Something Matthew said and the way he acted stopped me.

. . .

Mother Jordan came to Ginger's house and picked me up to go back home with her. We chattered on and on during our ride back to the farm and even sang some of Mother Jordan's favorite songs. Our talking rambled on, sometimes together, asking questions then answering. We arrived home before I knew it.

After dinner and feeding the few animals left on the farm, Mother Jordan and I sat and talked; she in her rocker, and me at her feet with my head on her lap. Her hands stroking my hair made me feel peaceful. She hummed softly. I fell asleep.

Two days later, I packed a few belongings in a feed sack and placed them on the table ready for the ride into town. My last morning was full of finishing touches in the barn. The hay was stacked for old Jeb, our mule, along with feed for our last cow. When I finally went inside the cabin, Mother Jordan stood by the table. She handed me a bag she had sewn. "It's for you to put your clothing in to take back and forth to Ginger's. You should have something nice to carry your things in."

As I ran my hand over the material, I began to cry. "It's so pretty." I recognized a piece of my first dress given to me by Mother Jordan, and one of Father Jordan's shirts, all pieces of material intricately sewn together to make a bag for me. "It's beautiful, Mother Jordan. Thank you. You are too good to me."

"Nonsense, child, you're my daughter and I want you to have something other than a feed sack for your belongings. Now let's hurry along; it's a long ride."

Mother Jordan took the reins and the wagon gave a jolt. I turned and looked at the now run-down cabin. It was beginning to be more than both of us could take care of. I wondered how much longer Mother Jordan would be able to stay out here by herself. Then I remembered the questions I wanted to ask. Before I could stop myself I blurted, "Mother Jordan, Matthew told me Ginger's girls let the men buy drinks for them and the girls sing for them. Why is that so bad? Matthew acted like it wasn't something I should see. I asked him to take me to the saloon to see for myself and he said no."

Mother Jordan pulled the wagon to a stop. Her face turned pale. She turned to me, "You listen to Matthew! If this is where Miss Ginger works, you have no business going to the saloon, now or any time."

With that said, she picked up the reins, gave Jeb a jerk, and proceeded to town. Mother Jordan's outburst startled me. Her tone told me not to ask any more questions and I'd better stay away, far away from the saloon. Now, from her outburst, I was forming a plan for a trip to the saloon, by myself. There was more to this than what they were telling me.

Mother Jordan and I said our goodbyes and I stood on the porch watching her drive away until I could no longer see the wagon. I turned to go in, but Ginger blocked the doorway. I hadn't heard the door open behind me.

"Good morning, Katie. I trust you had a nice visit with

your mother. I'm glad to see you back." She smiled and stood aside to let me pass.

"Good morning, Ginger. We had a nice visit. I'll start fixing your breakfast as soon as I put my clothes away." I headed to my room.

Ginger came into the kitchen as I began stoking the fire in the stove. "Delia went into work without me this morning. She had things to take care of for me. I'll be the only one to feed. Fix yourself a plate and join me. I hate eating alone."

I placed the flour, lard, and milk in a bowl and began mixing. "I'm not sure. Do you really want me to eat with you?"

"Of course, like I said, I don't like eating alone. Besides we can get to know each other better."

An hour later, I sat across from Ginger buttering my biscuit. "Thank you for letting me eat breakfast with you. This is nice."

"Nonsense, dear, it's about time we got to know each other a bit better. I heard you're a survivor of an Indian massacre. Is that right?"

Before I could stop it, the deep hidden memories flooded my mind. Memories I thought I'd forgotten until Ginger opened the box, my box of hidden treasures that I didn't want to share with anyone else. "I am, and now I live with my second family, Mother Jordan." I hoped this was going to be the only question she asked.

"What brought you to this town?" I asked. "Did you know anyone here?"

She took a bite of her eggs. "No, I didn't know anyone here, and this town is just as good as any other." Another bite of egg, "Delia and I decided this was the place for us.

We came from Louisiana."

"Is Louisiana a long ways away? I thought you said you were from the Carolinas."

She put her fork down and stared out the window for a long time. With her elbows on the table, she folded her hands and leaned on her chin. I thought she wasn't going to answer. She seemed so far away. *Maybe I shouldn't have asked that question.*

"Yes, I was born in the Carolinas but moved to Louisiana with Delia before coming here. And, yes, it is a long way from here. But when we saw this place, we knew this was where we needed to live. The people here have been friendly. As friendly as any other place we've been."

Ginger picked up her empty plate and took it to the kitchen. I followed, still not knowing very much about her or Delia. *Why did she work in a saloon? Maybe she'll tell me later.* I didn't know her well enough to keep asking personal questions, nor did I want her to get mad at me. My only hope of knowing the real Ginger, before I got more inquisitive, was to wait and get to know her better.

Ginger retreated to her room to get dressed for the day, and I returned to the kitchen to clean. My day had begun. In my mind, I began putting my plan together. I still wanted to see what no one was willing to tell me. Mother Jordan's outburst still troubled me. Matthew's reluctant answer about the saloon made me more determined to see Ginger's business in action. And following our breakfast conversation, I really felt like Ginger was holding something back about herself and Delia.

Chapter 26

Summer 1850

A week later, I overheard Ginger tell Delia this was going to be a busy night. This was payday for the miners; they received all their back pay too, and were on their way to town to relax. They both laughed, and even took longer than usual dressing, leaving later than they normally did for town.

My energy kept me busy cleaning, not once but twice, everything. I swept the front porch and straightened the rocking chairs. The flowers looked like they needed more water so I picked the bucket up and headed for the pump. With the water poured over the dry ground, it seemed like the flowers opened their buds even wider. Back in the house, I straightened the blankets on Ginger and Delia's beds again, and then paced the floors for hours.

Finally, a couple of hours after dark I found my chance to find out what the girls did at the saloon. I closed the door behind me and started for town. The dark sky held enough moon to light my way for the few blocks I had to go. As I got closer, I heard laughter and music. I kept to the shadows to keep from being seen by anyone. My hands started sweating. I've never done anything like this before.

Sounds of singing, laughter, and piano filled the air. I knew they were playing a piano because it sounded like the music I heard in church when we all went. Mother Jordan always liked the piano music.

From a few windows, I could see flickering lights. Most families in town lived above or behind their business. I wondered if they liked the music and singing interrupting their quiet evenings. Mother Jordan would not get used to the noise, nor would I.

I finally reached the saloon and saw the swinging doors with light shining above and below its opening. Men laughed, slapped each other on the back, and staggered in and out. Music filled the quiet street. I looked around and crept closer into the darkness, careful not to be seen. Slowly I slid against the building, staying in the shadows, and knelt down to look in the window.

It was so crowded...men everywhere. And women, a lot of women, and they wore very little. It looked like the underclothing I helped Ginger get into every day. The women sat on men's laps and stood behind them rubbing their backs. One woman was rubbing the man's head while holding his hat in her other hand. A man played the piano while two women sat and sang on top of the piano. These songs weren't familiar to me. Realization hit me...these were the girls I fixed meals for every day.

Then I spotted Ginger. I almost didn't recognize her. She wasn't wearing the dress she had on when she left the house earlier. In fact, I had never seen this dress before. Her usual dress was high on her neck. This one was bright green, and highlighted her smooth, silky skin and her ample bust with its low cut. Her beautiful red hair was piled high on her head with white beads intertwined with each curl. Several men stood close to her talking. I didn't see Delia.

Then I heard the sound of wood splitting. My head jerked toward the front door as a man flew through the swinging doors and landed in the street. Two men ran out behind him and lunged for him. Quickly I slipped back into the shadows of the building, out of sight. The two men picked the other one up and punched him. When he fell backwards, they continued hitting and kicking him. The man fell to the ground and didn't move. My hand flew to my mouth to keep from making a noise. Both men went back inside assured they'd taken care of him.

It seemed like a long time, but I'm sure it wasn't, as I watched the man slowly stagger to his feet and limp in my direction. I backed away to the back of the building, trying not to make a sound. He kept coming; I kept backing up. He fell at my feet. I waited to see if he would get up before I bent down to roll him over. When I did, I saw his face was bruised and bloody. I knelt down and I used my skirt to wipe some of the blood away. Curly black hair framed his face. My fingers traced the fine lines on his fair skin, over the bridge of his small nose. He moved. I sprung to my feet as he turned over and tried to get up. I knew I couldn't be caught here in town, so I raised my skirt and turned to run; he moaned. Once more, I turned to look at him as he raised his head; then I ran. Scared, I ran as fast as I could, hoping no one would follow. By the time I reached the house, I was out of breath. I fell down on the porch, only a minute, I thought, so I could catch my breath before entering the house. I stood at the door with my hand on the knob listening for any sounds. When I felt sure I was alone, I headed for my room and sat down on the bed. Then

I noticed the blood on the bottom of my skirt.

Jumping up, I ran to the kitchen and poured a pan of water. My hands shook as I slipped out of my dress. I laid it on the worktable and began scrubbing. Ginger couldn't know I was in town. I had to get the blood out of my dress before she got home.

Chapter 27

Summer 1850

A week later, Ginger, Delia, and I went to the mercantile to buy supplies. Ginger never asked me anything about the night I slipped into town. Little did I know how short-lived my relief would be. If she started asking questions, I was apprehensive about being able to convince her I was just curious, although I still had many questions.

Upon entering the door of the store, the smell of coffee grounds, musty wood, and cigar smoke filled my nostrils. For a minute I stood breathing it all in. Sometimes the cigar smoke reminded me of the pipe my father smoked when the men gathered. And how could I forget Father Jordan's pipe. He always let me put the tobacco in it for him.

Pointing to the corner of the store, Mr. Goodnight said, "New bolts of cloth just arrived."

Without thinking of anything else, I started toward the cloth.

Ginger chimed in. "Pick out something you like, Katie. The hems of your skirts have been looking pretty tattered and stained lately."

I stopped short. My neck and face felt flushed. Ginger knew. I continued to the cloth without looking back. My hand ran across the prettiest green plaid I'd ever seen. It reminded me of the green dress Ginger wore that night. Immediately my thoughts flew back to the sound of the piano and women singing. I jumped when Ginger placed her hand over mine.

"Pretty, isn't it? I've always liked the color green." She batted her eyes. "Do you think it matches my eyes?"

Her hand felt like lead. Slowly I pulled my hand free. I tried to smile. "Yes, the material does match the color of your eyes." Maybe she doesn't know.

She picked up the bolt and proceeded to the counter. "Mr. Goodnight, would you please put this on my account along with the rest of our goods? If Mrs. Goodnight is not too busy, do you think she would be able to put a dress together for Katie?" She turned and winked.

He took it from her hands and laid it down behind him. "Of course, Miss Ginger. I'll talk to the Mrs. I'm sure she'll be able to fit it in. I can let you know." He leaned closer to Ginger and said in a lower voice, not quite a whisper, but I heard every word. "Miss Ginger, there was a gentleman in here two days ago asking if I knew a woman who wore white moccasins. I told him no, but I was wondering if your Katie might have met him?"

"What did this man look like?"

He cleared his throat. "I think he was German, medium build. It was hard to understand him. Said he hadn't been in this country very long. Looked like he'd been in a bit of a tussle, He still had bruises and cuts about the face. He never did say why he was looking for her. I just thought you might like to know, never can be too careful these days."

Ginger whirled around and looked at me for a good minute, one eyebrow raised. I froze. She turned back to Mr.

Goodnight. "That sounds like the man who got into a row with two of the miners about a week ago, roughed him up pretty good. Never did hear what started it as it was over quickly. Well, it's probably nothing. Will you have Matthew bring our supplies out to the house?"

"Yes, of course. Well, have a good day, ladies."

• • •

We walked home in silence. As soon as the door closed, I headed to my room. Then I heard Ginger clear her throat. I stopped, frozen, waiting.

"Katie, could I have a word with you?"

I turned and stood, waiting.

Ginger stood opposite me with her arms crossed over her chest. She looked at me in a way that made me think I should tell her what had happened. "Is there something you have to tell me?"

Here it comes. I wasn't good at lying and I knew she would be able to tell it if I tried. I looked down at the floor and rubbed my hands together. "Ginger, it was nothing, really it wasn't. I just wanted to see the girls...where they worked, what you did in town, and—"

Her hearty laugh stopped me.

She clapped. "Oh, my dear girl, you should have said something. If you wanted to know, I would have taken you to meet the girls; although, I don't believe your mother would approve. Come over here and sit down. Tell me what happened."

We both sat at the table. Delia went into the kitchen and I could hear her rattling around with the stove and dishes. "I really didn't want to disobey anyone, but I just wanted to see what Matthew wouldn't tell me. And Mother

Jordan wouldn't tell me anything."

"Matthew? How did he get involved?"

I leaned back in my chair. The words came rushing. "The night Matthew came for the girls' dinner I asked him where they worked and what they did. He said you and the girls worked at the saloon, and that men paid to sit with the girls and buy them drinks. Then he wouldn't tell me anything else. I felt like there was more and I wanted to know."

Delia brought the teapot with cups and saucers. Her face showed no emotion when she placed them on the table and went into her bedroom. I wondered why she was being so quiet. *Had she been listening? Perhaps she could hear better from her room.* I looked back to Ginger. "I asked Mother Jordan what the girls did in the saloon, but she got angry and wouldn't answer me."

Ginger poured the tea. "Katie, what Matthew told you is true. The men do buy the girls drinks and the girls do sit with the men. That's all you need to know. But, you haven't told me how you know this man who is looking for you."

"Oh, that." I dipped my spoon in the sugar bowl then added it to my tea giving it a leisurely stir. "One week ago, I waited until after you and Delia left for work, then late in the evening I slipped into town. I watched the girls through the window, singing, drinking, and dancing. Then a man crashed through the swinging doors along with two other men chasing him. The two men beat him up pretty bad. I thought he was dead until he got up and came to where I was hiding. He fell at my feet." I took a sip of my tea. "I shook him and said 'Mister' a couple of times but he didn't answer. When I turned him over, I saw blood all over his face so I tried to clean it off with my skirt. He moaned. I got scared and ran. That's all that happened. I'm telling you the truth, really I am. I don't know who he was, or what his name is."

Ginger stood up, came around the table, and put her arms around me. "I believe you, Katie. I'm just glad you're all right and nothing happened to you. I'll do some checking in town and see why he wants to find you. You've had a trying day, why not go in and take a nap." She chuckled. "I don't believe your mother will approve of your romp, and I'm not going to lie to her about your escapade, although, I'll have to tell her if she asks. Now don't worry, you've done nothing wrong, except of course, going into town without my knowledge. I trust this won't happen again." She scowled.

My voice came out in a whisper. "No, it won't." I turned to leave.

Ginger interrupted my thoughts before I reached the kitchen door. "Katie, I've been meaning to ask. You don't have to answer if you don't want to, but I was wondering why you wear moccasins."

I turned and smiled. "It makes me feel closer to my family. That's all I have left of them. When I put them on in the morning, I can almost feel my mother's presence."

"That sounds lovely."

"Besides, my feet hurt when I wear white man's shoes."

She laughed. "Now that really makes sense, sometimes I don't know how my feet can stand wearing them all day."

• • •

One week turned into two, then three. Between cleaning Ginger's house and fixing meals, I'd almost forgotten about the man who was looking for me. No one spoke about him, almost as if he never existed. I was beginning to question his existence myself.

I was in my bedroom putting my nightgown in my bag to go home with Mother Jordan when I heard the front door slam shut. Ginger rushed into my room out of breath, as if she had run all the way from the saloon. She grabbed me by both shoulders.

"You'll never believe what happened just a few minutes ago. I stopped by the general store to pick up your dress Mrs. Goodnight finished. That man was standing there talking to Mr. Goodnight, and he asked about the girl in the moccasins again." She stopped to catch her breath. "Mr. Goodnight looked past him at me. The man turned to see who Mr. Goodnight was looking at. Oh, my goodness, Katie, he was the same man I saw in the saloon a few weeks ago that the two miners had the ruckus with." She fanned her face with her hand. "I wondered what had happened to him. I thought he left town." She finally sat down on my bed.

"Did he say anything to you?" I asked.

"Let me catch my breath, dear girl."

I went to get her a glass of water from the kitchen. Upon my return, she was still fanning her face. "Here, drink some of this." I handed her the glass.

Ginger took a long drink and set the glass down on my bedside table. "Well, Katie, let me see, where to begin. Oh my." She took a long breath and sat up straight. "When he turned and looked at me, I guess he recognized me from the saloon. He approached and extended his hand introducing himself as Probus Eberle. Oh, and his eyes, Katie, he has the prettiest eyes I've ever seen, so clear."

I sat down beside her, now wanting to hear more. "Did

he say anything else?"

"He cleared his throat. Then in broken English he asked me if I knew the girl who wore white moccasins."

"I wasn't sure how to answer him at first, but he seemed so open and sincere. So I told him I did."

My heart jumped two feet. I felt like I should grab it and put it back in my chest. "Did he say why?"

The sounds of a wagon pulling up to the house interrupted us. I ran to the window to see Mother Jordan coming to a stop in front. I watched her get down from the wagon. "It's Mother Jordan."

Ginger stood behind me. "Let's keep this conversation to ourselves. I don't think your mother would be pleased with your going into town. We'll discuss it further when you return."

"Yes, Miss Ginger. I won't say anything."

With my bag packed and ready to go, I grabbed it and headed to the door before Mother Jordan could knock.

Mother Jordan couldn't get a word in edgewise as I chatted all the way to the farm. "Ginger bought some new material and had a dress made for me. She picked it up today from Mrs. Goodnight, and it's really pretty. I tried it on and it fits just right. It's green like one of Ginger's dresses. Did you know her green dress matches her eyes?" I was about to run out of things to talk about when we pulled up to the house. "You go on in and let me take care of the horse and wagon. You look tired."

She turned and looked deep into my eyes. I always felt like she saw my very soul. My weight shifted and I grabbed the reins. "Let me get down first, and then I'll help you."

"My goodness girl, you've bantered all the way home. Guess you tired me out by everything you've been doing. I'll see you in the house after you put up old Jeb."

Relief flooded over me…at least for now. I knew I had to keep quiet about the man in town. Mother Jordan would never approve of what I did, and now the man wants to meet me. Still, I wondered. *What kind of a man is he? Why does he want to meet me?*

It felt good to be home even if only one night. I ran my hand over the back of the mule and patted him on the rump. "Jeb, I wished you could talk. I could tell you about this man in town, then, you could tell me how to tell Mother Jordan." He turned his head to look at me, then back to the hay I'd put down. He snorted.

I headed to the door. The old barn showed more wear than I remembered. A few more boards needed replacing and a fresh coat of white wash. Even though I'd only been gone for a few months, it seemed like the farm was falling into more disrepair every time I came home. I knew Mother Jordan would never leave the farm. Still, she would be much more comfortable living with one of the girls, than being out here all by herself. If I could only think of the right words to say to her.

I looked around the barn again to see if I'd missed something, further delaying talking with Mother Jordan. Surely, she could still read my thoughts.

The sun settled behind the trees, and shadows became larger. I couldn't dilly dally any longer. I strolled over to the chicken coop to gather some eggs and then checked on the sow beside the barn, just to make sure she had enough feed.

"Katie, are you coming in?"

Mother Jordan's voice snapped me back to reality. It was time to go in. I told myself not to think of what went on in town. Maybe if I didn't think about it, I wouldn't let anything slip. *That's what I'm going to do. Not think about town.*

"Coming, Mother Jordan."

We sat opposite each other, and between bites of fried potatoes and cornbread, we made small talk. "Mother Jordan, I noticed the barn is looking pretty run down. Maybe I could find someone in town to come out and help repair some of the boards."

She put her fork down. "Nonsense child, that old barn is fine. It'll last another ten years or so. But, I am interested in what is going on with your job. Are you doing all right?"

"Oh, yes. Everything is fine." I chewed, and then wiped my mouth. *Think quickly.* I almost choked stuffing so much cornbread in my mouth to keep from talking.

Mother Jordan put her hands on each side of her plate and sat silent. The silence unnerved me. I looked up from my plate to see her staring at me.

"When are you going to tell me what's going on? You were chatting nonstop all the way home and now you're reluctant to answer my question. Is there something I should know?"

"No."

She sat back in her chair and put her hands in her lap. *Oh no. Please, not that long stare. Ginger said it would be our secret. How am I going to do that--?*

Mother Jordan pushed her chair back and got up. She picked up the dishes and took them to the sideboard. "Well, Katie, I'm sure you're going to tell me, I just don't know when."

Now I've really done it. I've hurt her feelings.

"Mother Jordan, there isn't anything going on. I'm

glad to be home with you, even if it's for one day. I guess I was trying to tell you everything I'd been doing, and I got carried away. I wanted you to share my days, too." I kissed her cheek and took the dishes from her. "You go sit down; I'll take care of these. You look tired."

She raised an eyebrow and handed me the plates. "Now if I listen to you much longer you'll have me bedridden. I've taken care of everything around the farm, and I don't feel a bit tired." She smiled and winked. "But, take the dishes, and I'll go sit in my chair. I do have a couple of things to mend."

With a sigh of relief, I turned and took the dishes to the counter, cleaned them, and put them away. When I finished, I sat down at the feet of Mother Jordan and watched her nimble fingers as she sewed a tear on her one good dress. "I wish I could buy you a new dress for church. This one's faded and worn thin from so many washings. I don't think you've had a new dress since Father Jordan passed away."

"Dear child, now where am I going to wear a new dress?" She smiled and rubbed my cheek.

"But, it's not right. Ginger had a new dress made for me because mine was stained." I caught myself as soon as I said stained. I yawned and stood up. "I'm tired. It's been a long day. I think we both should turn in." I kissed her on the forehead and quickly headed toward my room.

Mother Jordan furrowed her forehead. "Now, how did your dress get stained so quickly?"

I continued toward my room. "It was probably all the cooking and cleaning I do for Ginger and her girls." I closed the door and leaned against it, hoping that answer sufficed.

Mother Jordan must have gone to bed right after me because the house grew quiet very quickly. The only sound

I heard was the whistling of the wind through the trees and the thin walls of the cabin. Occasionally, one of the tree branches brushed against the window. Almost like it was tapping out a message, a message reminding me how I hadn't told Mother Jordan all the truth.

Chapter 28

Fall 1850

A month passed and I still felt tension between Mother Jordan and myself every time I went home. Like Ginger said, my encounter in town would be our secret, but it grew harder to hide every time I looked at Mother Jordan.

One sunny morning, Ginger and Delia sat at the table finishing their breakfast when I noticed a man walking toward the house. "Miss Ginger, someone's coming."

She stood up, tied her housecoat loosely around her waist, and walked to the door. Delia followed.

Ginger pulled the curtain aside. "Delia, go get the shotgun. I don't recognize him. Can't be too careful."

By the time Delia returned with the shotgun, the man had stepped onto the porch. Ginger turned and looked in my direction. "Katie, go to your room. Now."

I turned and ran. I closed the door behind me, then opened it just enough to hear what was being said.

Ginger yelled, "Mister, that's far enough. State your business or you'll be wearing this shotgun."

I heard him say something like "Halt, Halt." I couldn't hear anything else, so I slid the door open a little bit more. Their voices were still too low. I inched my way along the wall to the door leading into the living room. Ginger put the gun down by her side and spoke to him through the screen door. I couldn't hear what she said. Delia stood next to Ginger with her arms crossed. Ginger opened the screen door, and the man entered. His tall lanky frame filled the doorway. I backed up so no one could see me. With my mind fixed on the man, I suddenly tripped over the water bucket. When I tried to stop myself from falling, I grabbed the hot pot on top of the stove. "Ouch." The pot flew into the air, and I fell backwards knocking more pots off their stand.

All three came running into the kitchen to see what happened. I was sprawled on my backside on the floor, rubbing my burned hand. My skirts, wrapped halfway up my legs, left my white moccasins quite noticeable to everyone.

Pointing, the man said, "Ja, ja, the white moccasins. You are the one. I have found you." He reached for my hand to pull me up.

Ginger laid her hand on his shoulder and reached for me. He retracted his hand and watched as I stood up. His face looked familiar, but I couldn't place him. Not that I knew many men in town, but I saw a few men at the general store when I went with Mother Jordan or Ginger.

Still nursing my blistered hand, I headed toward the table to put butter on it. Mother Jordan always said if you have a burn, rub butter on it, and it won't blister.

"Brush yourself off, Katie," Ginger said. "Then please come into the living room so we can have a talk with our guest."

"Yes, Miss Ginger." Just a few minutes before, she was going to shoot him. Now she was calling him her guest. I wondered what made her change her mind. The man turned and followed Ginger into the living room mumbling something I didn't understand. He did have pretty eyes, the color of root beer barrels, my favorite candy, from Mr. Goodnight's store. I rubbed my aching hand again.

"Katie, are you coming?" Ginger called.

"Yes, Miss Ginger," Before she could call me again, I sat down beside her at the table.

Haltingly, the man fumbled with his words. "You have the white moccasins, ja, you are the one in the alley, no? The one who tried to help me."

I looked at Ginger then back to him.

"Go ahead, Katie. It's all right." Ginger patted my hand. "This is Mr. Eberle. He is new here, only been in the country for two years. You can talk to him. He wants to let you know he's grateful for your help." She looked to Mr. Eberle. "Mr. Eberle, this is Katie, my housekeeper."

"Ja, ja. I am pleased to meet you, Katie." His smile felt warm and inviting and when he nodded, a tiny black curl fell to his forehead and bounced. Now his eyes reminded me of Jeb, our old mule, after I brushed him.

"You're welcome." I wanted to say more but couldn't think of anything.

He turned to Ginger. "Miss Ginger, my English is not good, but I wish to say how sorry I am for the night of the fight in your saloon." He lowered his head and went on. "I will pay for any damages I have caused."

Ginger laughed. "Well, now, you're the first to come out and want to pay for damages. I usually have to track them down or bar them from my place until they pay up. But, Mr. Eberle, your fight went outside before I knew there was any fight going on. There were no damages inside. I'm just glad to see you're all right." She turned to me. "Isn't that right, Katie?"

Everyone looked at me. I could feel my face warm. No man had ever looked at me like that. I liked it. "Yes." Now, I felt embarrassed. *Can't I say anything else?* Something about this man made my stomach feel like tiny butterflies flittering about.

Delia had been quiet during our conversation. She stood up and smoothed her skirt. "Excuse me, please. Let me get some hot water and fresh cups for tea." She turned and disappeared into the kitchen.

Ginger cleared her throat. "Mr. Eberle, I appreciate you coming out here to thank my Katie, and wanting to pay for some damages to my place. But, I'm thinking there may be another reason for your visit."

Mr. Eberle looked at Ginger, and then rested his gaze on me. "Ja, Miss Ginger. I would like to know Miss Katie better. That is, with your permission."

Even in his broken English, I understood what he was asking. He wanted to know me. Now my stomach really started quivering. I remember when Andrew wanted to spend time with Mary Ann, and when James courted Amanda. Everyone sat around the fire, played games, and talked. Sometimes I went on buggy rides with Amanda and James when they went on picnics. Mother Jordan said they needed a chaperone. Now, I would need a chaperone. My heart raced. Ginger brought me back to reality when she interrupted my thoughts.

"You know, Mr. Eberle, Katie's mother lives about three miles from here. She goes there once a week to spend a couple of days with her. You'll have to get her permission, besides mine." She smiled at me. "Of course, if Mrs. Jordan does not give her permission, there's nothing I can do."

We sat in silence for a moment letting that bit of information sink in. Delia brought our hot tea and set it down. "I thought you might like some of the cookies Katie made. They go quite well with the tea." After pouring, she sat down and joined us. Her stern face told me nothing of what she might be thinking. Her tightly pulled back, never out of place hair, made her look older. I had guessed her to be older than Ginger but didn't really know. Then again, Ginger hadn't revealed her age either.

Mr. Eberle broke the silence. "Miss Ginger, when is the next day Katie goes home? Perhaps I could be here to meet her mother." He reached for his second cookie. "These are very good."

"Well now, that was quick." Ginger laughed. "Yes, Katie is a very good cook. And you don't waste any time. Mrs. Jordan will be here in two days. I can make sure I'm here when she comes to introduce you."

"Thank you." He stood up and bowed. "I will be here in two days. I must excuse myself for I am a hired hand on Mr. Klingman's farm. Again, thank you for the tea and cookies." He smiled at me. "I will see you in two days, Katie."

We all followed him to the door then watched as he walked down the road. With my fingers on the screen, I traced his outline.

Ginger rubbed my back. "It looks like he'll be courting you, young lady. I do hope Mrs. Jordan has no objections."

Delia picked up the dishes and headed toward the kitchen. "Let me get those for you," I said to Delia. "Thank you for the tea. Don't you both have to get ready for work?"

Ginger yawned. "This has been a lazy morning, but a very exciting one, too. Katie has a beau." She stretched and yawned again. "Delia, we have work to do. It's payday for some of the miners. I'm off to get ready."

"I'm right behind you," Delia said.

"I'm in the kitchen. I'll have your meals ready when you return, Delia." I almost danced as I shook out the tablecloth, replaced the sugar bowl, salt and pepper, and headed to the kitchen. My hand stung as I put it in the hot dishwater. I had almost forgotten I had burned it earlier. I gazed out the window, watching two rabbits hop across the dry, dusty road. A slight breeze bristled the leaves across the window.

My mind sped. *He was beaten and bloody in the dark alley that night. No wonder I don't recognize his face. But, he remembered my moccasins. Now he wants to court me. He'll have to visit me during the day when Ginger and Delia are home. How am I going to tell Mother Jordan? Mother Jordan just has to like him... I like him.*

Chapter 29

Fall 1850

Two days later, as the sun climbed over the horizon, Mr. Eberle arrived. My heart sped up as Miss Ginger's clock chimed seven times. I opened the door; he tipped his worn hat and said, "Guten Morgen, Fräulein Katie. This is good day, no?" His eyes twinkled when he smiled.

My heart fluttered and I felt light headed as I put my finger to my lips. "Quiet. Miss Ginger and Delia are still asleep."

"No, we're not, Mr. Eberle." She approached the door. "I told you, we'd be here when you arrived, and we will be here to introduce you to Mrs. Jordan. Come in and have some tea with us. Or perhaps you'd prefer coffee? Katie's coffee is the best here on the Mississippi." She tightened her robe and sat down at the table.

He took off his hat and shook his boots before entering. "No, Miss Ginger, tea will be fine. Please, my name is Probus. Mr. Eberle sounds like you're talking to my father."

My face reddened, and my stomach had those same butterflies flying about. I made my way to the kitchen to heat water, and Mr. Eberle followed. I gestured at a chair for him to sit. Even though he said he only wanted tea this morning, I began my routine of preparing breakfast for Ginger and Delia. My concentration waned as Mr. Eberle sat only a few feet from me, making it difficult to make the biscuits.

Mother Jordan would be here in no time, and all my thoughts of being courted would be dashed. I knew she wouldn't be happy about it, especially since she didn't know him. And when she found out how I met him... *No matter what I tell her, no amount of explaining will be enough.*

I returned to the parlor where Ginger and Delia sat. Mr. Eberle followed me again. "Please sit, Mr. Eberle," Ginger said.

I set the platter of biscuits, eggs, and ham before everyone and then sat down to eat. I watched as Mr. Eberle placed several biscuits along with three eggs and two slices of ham on his plate.

"Smells gut." He took a bite. "And tastes gut, too."

Miss Ginger laughed. "I'm glad you like Katie's cooking."

Delia sat stone-faced, making her thoughts hard to read. She never said much, but she was always there, beside Ginger. *I wish I knew more about her.*

So far, nothing about this morning seemed usual. Mr. Eberle sat across from me and wanted to get permission to court me. My stomach churned, and my throat tightened. I couldn't eat another bite. My head swam, drowning out all external sounds.

"Katie, I hear a wagon." Miss Ginger nudged my shoulder.

"What, what did you say?"

"You must be deep in thought, young lady," Miss Ginger said. "I think I hear Mrs. Jordan's wagon." She stood up.

The chair fell over when I stood. Mr. Eberle came

around the table and picked it up. We both reached the door together behind Ginger, about the time the wagon came to a stop.

Ginger turned to me. "Well, you best get out there, Katie. Probus, you stay here. At least until Mrs. Jordan comes in." She motioned to Delia. "Delia, would you clear the table and get some fresh hot water? We'll probably need a big pot of tea."

I bounded out the door and down the steps as Mother Jordan tied the mule to the rail. When she turned, I threw my arms around her neck. "Mother Jordan, I'm so glad to see you. Come in, have some breakfast. You probably didn't eat a bite before you left."

Mother Jordan leaned back and looked at me. "I could eat one of your biscuits. You know, you do make some good biscuits." She gave me a kiss on the cheek and rubbed my back.

I opened the door then followed her in. Everyone stood when we entered. I saw Mother Jordan's back stiffen. My stomach tightened.

"Mrs. Jordan, please sit down. Katie fixed the biscuits you like so well, and Delia has fresh hot water for tea." Ginger motioned to a chair. "Please, you're probably hungry from your ride into town."

Mother Jordan walked over to the table, looking first to Ginger then to Mr. Eberle. "A cup of tea would be fine, and maybe one biscuit." She sat down.

Before anyone spoke, Delia brought the platter back to the table with the rest of the biscuits. She returned to the kitchen for the tea. I sat down next to Mother Jordan. She cleared her throat.

Miss Ginger began. "Mrs. Jordan, I'd like you to meet

Mr. Probus Eberle."

Mr. Eberle stood up. "Frau Jordan." He stepped toward her and extended his hand.

Mother Jordan shook his hand. "Mr. Eberle."

Silence filled the air. Delia returned with the teapot and began pouring.

"Mother Jordan, I—"

"Mrs. Jordan, Katie—"

"Frau Jordan, I'm pleased—"

Mother Jordan put her hand up. "I can tell, or rather I can see, something is going on here. Miss Ginger, you begin, please."

"Mother Jordan," I began.

"Katie, I said Miss Ginger. You'll have your chance."

I folded my hands and put them in my lap. I knew better than to say anything more when I heard Mother Jordan's stern voice.

Ginger looked at Mr. Eberle then back to Mother Jordan. "Well, Mrs. Jordan, Mr. Eberle here has asked me if he could see your Katie. I told him first he had to get your permission."

Mother Jordan looked Mr. Eberle over more intently. "I see." She took a sip of tea.

I watched him as he eyed her. "Frau Jordan, I am honorable man. I wish to court, as you say, Miss Katie."

No one spoke. Finally, Mother Jordan asked, "Where did you meet my daughter?"

With a solemn face, he began. "About a month ago, two men beat me. Katie tried to help, but when I tried to thank her, she ran away. I searched for her to tell her thank you. Now that I found her, I want to know her better."

Mother Jordan turned to me. "Katie, why didn't you tell

me about this? Where did you meet him again?"

I swallowed. "Mother Jordan, I'm sorry." I looked at Ginger, and she nodded. "I slipped into town one night to see where Miss Ginger worked. I looked through the saloon window and saw the girls that work for her, and the men that buy the girls drinks, the singing, and—"

"Stop." Mother Jordan stood up. "I told you, no! I forbade you to go to the saloon."

"Frau Jordan," Mr. Eberle said.

Mother Jordan turned to him. "Young man, I told my daughter to stay away from the saloon, and now I find she disobeyed me. I will not have her around the likes of men who frequent the saloon. No. Katie, get your things, you're going home with me. Now!"

I'm a good girl. I didn't do anything wrong. I felt like a whole plate of cornbread and a gallon of sweet milk had been dumped into my stomach, hitting bottom all at once. "Mother Jordan, please, let me explain."

Mother Jordan's face reddened. "No. I told you before not to go around the saloon. No good comes from the saloon. I can't believe this is where Miss Ginger works. No. Get your things." She turned and walked out the door.

I sat down and covered my face. My world was spiraling. I didn't want to leave. Not now, I wanted to know Mr. Eberle better. I liked taking care of Miss Ginger and Delia, but my heart said Mother Jordan is my mother. She and Father Jordan rescued me and had been my parents for almost all my life. Tears spilled down my cheeks.

Mr. Eberle looked at Miss Ginger and me then headed for the door. I heard him say. "Frau Jordan, please, your Katie did nothing wr—"

"Katie, get out here, now," she yelled "One last time, or

I'm leaving."

Miss Ginger put her hand on my shoulder. "Honey, maybe you should go with your mother. Work things out, and then come back. Your job will be here waiting for you."

"But, Miss Ginger, I don't know if I want to go," I said through a sob. "I know I should." Hiccup. "But I like it here, too. I like Mr. Eberle." Hiccup. "I don't want to make my mother angry, but—"

I heard the crack of the reins hitting the wagon, "Hehaw," Mother Jordan yelled.

I jumped up and ran out the door to see the wagon flying down the road, faster than I'd ever seen it go before. Mother Jordan bounced on the seat, and rocks sprayed in the air from the wagon wheels. *What is she doing?* I watched in horror as the wagon hit a rut, lost a wheel, and turned over.

Mr. Eberle, Miss Ginger and I jumped off the porch and ran toward the wagon. Poor old Jeb's reins broke loose; he stopped as soon as the wagon turned over. By the time we arrived, Jeb stood over Mother Jordan's lifeless body. I fell down beside her and lifted her head. Between sobs, "No, no. Mother, no. I'm so sorry. This can't be happening. No."

Mr. Eberle picked up Mother Jordan in his strong arms and headed back to the house. I grabbed Jeb and followed with Miss Ginger by my side. Tears blinded my vision, and I tripped over rocks on the road.

Ginger finally took the mule from me and pushed me ahead of her. "Get up there with Mr. Eberle. I'll take care of the mule. Go on."

I nodded and quickened my pace, reaching him when he stepped on the porch. Delia opened the door and pointed. "Take her to my room."

Mr. Eberle laid Mother Jordan's still body on Delia's

bed. He turned and slipped out. I untied her bonnet and the first few buttons on her dress. Delia handed me a wet towel and I began wiping her face. "Mother Jordan," I whispered. "Please wake up. Don't leave me."

Miss Ginger and Delia stood behind me. Soon Mr. Eberle joined us with a pan of cool water. I rinsed the towel and wiped Mother Jordan's face again. No reaction. I looked at Ginger. "Are you sure she's breathing?"

Delia leaned closer to Mother Jordan's face. "Yes, she's breathing. Sometimes with a fall like this, the wind is knocked out of you. I'm sure she'll be all right. Maybe we should leave you alone with her, and we can wait in the other room. Call one of us, and we'll come back in to check on you." She turned and gently pushed the other two out of the room.

"No, wait. Should we get Doc to come? She has a large lump on her forehead. Maybe she hit a rock. "I pushed her hair back. "I don't see any more cuts or bumps."

Miss Ginger walked back into the room. She pushed Mother Jordan's hair back from her forehead again. "Oh, dear, I think maybe you're right. I'll have Delia run over to Doc's office and fetch him."

Mr. Eberle poked his head in the doorway. "Miss Ginger, I need to go over to Mr. Klingman's place. I'll stop by Doc's and ask him to come by. I'm sorry to rush out, but we have one load of hay to bring in before it rains." He tipped his hat to me. "I'm sorry, Miss Katie."

Ginger met Mr. Eberle at the door and walked out with him. I heard the screen door close. The house was quiet except for Mother Jordan's shallow breathing. The slow rise and fall of her chest mesmerized me. My thoughts wandered back to the first time I laid eyes on her. I could almost hear the swishing noise her dress made as she walked. *We've come so far together, and now...How did it happen? Am I so selfish to want my own way? Mother Jordan has given me so much.* I sat on the floor and leaned my head on the bed as I held Mother Jordan's hand...*Don't fall asleep here. Great Spirit, please don't let Mother die.* I thought about Father Jordan. My parents, sisters, and Askuwheteau. It seemed like so long ago. Images of Mother Jordan sitting with her Good Book on her lap came to mind. I bowed my head in reverence to her ways. *Dear Father, please don't let Mother die.*

The sun peeked through the window when I awoke. My neck felt sore and stiff. Mother Jordan was still asleep. When I stood, I had the feeling of needles pricking my feet; it took a few minutes of massaging them to make the tingle go away. I noticed the grandfather clock on the wall. It was almost six o'clock. Miss Ginger and Delia would be home soon. I tried to be quiet as I made my way across the living room to the kitchen. Before I reached the kitchen door, Miss Ginger cleared her throat.

"I do hope we haven't disturbed you or your mother. How's she doing this morning?"

"Nothing, yet." I turned to look at her. "Are you just getting home?"

"No, dear, Delia went in to take care of things. I wanted to stay with you. Doc Barnes stopped by. You were so tired; we didn't want to disturb you, but we needn't have worried. You never stirred. Anyway, the doc said he'd be back later today to check on Mrs. Jordan. Until then, why don't you go lie down and let me sit with your mother." Ginger came over and rubbed my back. "My dear, your shoulders are stiff"

"I can't leave her, just in case she wakes up."

She rubbed my back and shoulders again. "I understand. You go lie down and don't worry about fixing meals today for Delia and me. Since Mother Jordan is in Delia's room, she'll get some sleep in my room. Then when Delia's rested, I'll go in and get a few winks. Until then, I'll sit with your mother while you sleep. Now run along." She gave me a shove toward my room.

"I'm going."

I must have been more tired than I thought because when I woke, my room was dark. My mind felt foggy. I flew off the bed and sprinted to Delia's room to see Mother. When I reached the door, I saw Ginger sitting beside her still body. "I'm sorry, Miss Ginger. I didn't mean to sleep so long."

"Nonsense child, come over here and sit with me." She patted the side of the bed. "Delia went to work tonight. I'll be staying here with you. Doc Barnes came while you were asleep and checked on your mother again. He said to keep her comfortable and continue hoping and waiting."

I sat down beside the bed, crossed my legs, and took Mother Jordan's hand. "I keep missing Doc Barnes. She's so still."

"Honey, I'm sure she'll be fine. I know it's scary to see her like this."

We sat in silence, alone in our own thoughts. As I looked at her, I wondered again, how Ginger ended up here. I wanted to know but I wasn't sure how to ask. Before I could stop the circling inner thoughts, the words tumbled out. "Miss Ginger, why did you come here? To this town?" My hand flew to my mouth. *Oh, my goodness, I said it. Now I've done it.*

Chapter 30

Fall 1830

Ginger didn't answer right away; in fact, I wasn't sure she would. Then, with a distant gaze, she began. "Oh, I'm not sure where to start. So many things have happened since that day." She grew quiet.

"What day?" I whispered, almost afraid I'd break the spell she seemed to be under.

She laid her hand over mine. "I pray your life will be blessed with much more than mine." She sighed. "It seems so long ago. We were so in love. We had each other, our plantation, and were looking forward to being parents."

"You were with child?"

"Yes, I was. I was due in two months." Her eyes watered. "We were thrilled. Our Indigo crop was abundant that year. This was our first shipment to England. Everything felt perfect."

"Indigo, what kind of crop is that?" My hand flew to my mouth. "I'm sorry, I didn't mean to interrupt."

"That's all right my dear. It's a plant used to dye material those beautiful colors you like so well. You know the ones I'm talking about, the different shades of bright blue to violet."

"I like the bright blues the best."

"Yes, I thought so." She chuckled. "But getting back to that day—Delia was helping me prepare things for the birth of our baby. We made a couple of small blankets, tiny night shirts, and bibs, and..."

"Delia was with you?"

"Yes, Delia and I have been together since the day her father came to our plantation looking for work. They were a sight, the two of them." She paused and took a deep breath. "Her mother had passed away in childbirth just before they arrived. Delia's father took his wife's death badly. He was withdrawn but a good worker. He tended the crop as if it were his own. And, his reputation as a carpenter grew. He made such lovely furniture to sell. Like I said, things were going well for all of us."

"But, what did Delia do while her father worked in the fields?"

Ginger cleared her throat. "Well, at first she stayed to herself. I suppose she grieved the loss of her mother and the only brother or sister she would ever have." She paused. "Then slowly but surely, Delia ventured up to the big house. I caught her taking care of my flowers on the porch one day and asked her if she'd like to come in and have tea."

"Did she?"

"Oh, yes, she came every day for tea. Then one thing led to another and before I knew it, she came early every morning and helped me with the house."

"She became your companion then?"

Mother Jordan stirred. Our attention turned to her immediately. She moved her head side to side but didn't wake.

"Where was I? Oh, yes, Delia became my constant

companion. She's two years younger than I, but at times, you'd think she was years older." Ginger stared at her dresser. "Then it happened. The day my world shattered. The day I wished I could forget, but it lingers, in my dreams almost every night."

"How old are you?"

"Silly child," Ginger said. "You must never ask a lady how old she is." She chided, holding her hand over her mouth. "But, I will tell you I was twenty at the time."

"I'm so sorry, Miss Ginger," I said blushing. "Please continue. It must have been very bad."

"My child, there wasn't anything anyone could have done. It happened so quickly." She took a deep breath. "It was a beautiful morning. Delia and I were in the kitchen preparing the noon meal when I heard gunshots. I dropped the scoop of flour; with Delia on my heels, we reached the door together. The smell of burning brush filled my nostrils. My husband and Delia's father were running from the burning fields with mounted riders close behind. As the guns fired, I saw workers in our fields fall." She paused as tears pooled in her eyes. "Then it happened. I watched as my Clay fell. Delia's father stopped, picked him up, and headed toward the house. He only took a few steps when the blow from a rider's, rifle butt struck him. I watched as another rider took aim and shot him." She dabbed her eyes with her handkerchief.

"You don't have to finish. It's too painful."

"No, I'll finish. Give me a minute." She began again, slowly. With each word she spoke, I could tell she was reliving the incident. "I ran down the steps to Clay. Delia tried to pull me back. I only took a few steps before the first rider hit me with his rifle. Everything went black. I don't remember anything until I woke up and found Delia sitting next to me rubbing my hands, her ashen face bleeding from a cut above her eye. I tried to get up but fell back. I went into labor." She rubbed her stomach. "I had my baby lying there in that smoke-filled Indigo field with my dead husband only a few feet from me. My precious little girl died before she took her first breath. I held her in my arms while I watched our home burn to the ground." She dabbed her eyes with the corners of her handkerchief. "If it hadn't been for Delia, I would have given up then. I was in shock and couldn't move. I don't remember much after that."

"Oh, Miss Ginger, I'm truly sorry for your loss." I rubbed her hand. "What happened to those men? Did you know them?"

"No, and no one in town knew them either. All we could figure was that it must have been a bunch of rowdy men bent on wreaking havoc for miles. I heard they finally met their match about a month after they destroyed my life." She stopped, and wrung her hands. "By then, all I thought about was leaving. My home, husband, and baby were gone. I had nothing left. After we buried our loved ones, I sold our land. Delia and I made plans to leave and go west, as far west as we could go. We ended up here. The friendly people of Flat Rock didn't ask a lot of questions, so we stayed."

"Miss Ginger, where was your plantation?"

"In the Carolinas. South Carolina. Not too far from the ocean, a perfect location for us. We were one of many plantations along the Atlantic." The faraway look came across her face again.

Before I could say anything, Ginger added, "And, no, I do not wish to marry again. Clay was the center of my life.

My one and only, no one could ever come close to taking his place. And I don't want anyone to take his place. End of story." She stood up, stretched, and walked out of the room.

She left me to my thoughts, to take in all she had just shared with me. I knew senseless cruelty, too, watching my family die. My heart strangely skipped a beat, and I thought about Mr. Eberle. *He wants to court me.* I shook my head trying to free myself of those selfish thoughts. I knew I should be thinking of my mother.

Chapter 31

Fall 1850

"I fixed some biscuits for you," Ginger said as she stepped inside the room. "You've been sitting by Mrs. Jordan's side all night. You really need to keep up your strength. Go in and eat. I'll sit here until you return."

"What if she wakes?"

"Don't argue. Go."

I had taken a few bites of the eggs and biscuits when I heard Ginger's voice.

"Katie, come quick."

The chair fell over as I jumped up. When I reached the door, I saw Mother Jordan's eyes open. I fell on my knees beside her bed.

Ginger stroked her face with a wet towel.

Mother Jordan blinked, like she was trying to focus.

"Mother Jordan, I'm here," I said.

She tried to sit up, but Ginger gently pushed her back down. "Mrs. Jordan, you've got a nasty bump on the head. You need to rest a bit before you try to sit up. Let me get you something to drink."

I sat down beside Mother. "You gave me a scare; I'm sorry I made you so angry. Really I am."

She didn't say anything, only looked at me. I started to squirm, anxious for her to say something. I rubbed her hands.

She turned her head and stared. "Where am I?"

"You're in Delia's bedroom at Miss Ginger's. Mr. Eberle sent Doc Barnes out to check on you, and he said you've got a big bump on your head that may take a few days to mend." I was sorry immediately that I said Mr. Eberle's name.

"Yes, yes, Mr. Eberle. Where is he?"

I wasn't sure how to answer her. "Well, he said he'd be back, but he didn't want his presence to upset you. He sent word with Miss Ginger that he would wait until you felt better before he came back."

"Oh." She tried sitting up again, but fell back on the bed. "Oh dear, I guess I'll lie here for a few minutes."

Miss Ginger returned with a glass of water and a cup of hot tea. I propped Mother Jordan up just enough so she could take a sip of tea, and then laid her back down. "Ginger, do you think she should eat something? She hasn't eaten anything in two days."

Ginger looked at Mother Jordan. "Do you think you could eat something? I don't think it would hurt if you had just a bite, just not a big meal anyway."

"If you bring me something, I'll try."

"I'll get it," I said and ran into the kitchen, buttered a biscuit, and placed a small teaspoon of jelly on a plate, just like she liked it. When I reached her room, she was trying to sit up again. Ginger's attention focused on the pan of water sitting on top of the dresser. "Mother Jordan, please let someone help you."

"I'll be all right." She sighed.

I set the plate on the chair. "I know, but let us, let me take care of you now. You always take care of everyone else. It's my turn now."

She lay back down and turned her head toward me. She was quiet for a long time.

"I think you two will be fine for a while," Ginger said. "I'm going to take a nap. If you need anything, come wake me, please."

"I can handle Mother Jordan." I smiled at Mother. "She's not going anywhere for a while."

"Katie?" Her voice sounded low and weak.

I bent closer to her. "Mother Jordan, I'll sit with you. Rest now, so you can get back on your feet. Maybe you'd like a bite of the biscuit I brought you?"

She shook her head. "Child, I feel so foolish. I behaved badly in front of you and everyone. Can you forgive me?"

"There's nothing to forgive. I just want you to get well."

She seemed reassured for she looked at the ceiling then closed her eyes. Her even breathing told me she had fallen asleep. *Sleep is good for her. Healing, just like the Doc said.*

. . .

"Katie?"

I sat up quickly rubbing my face and eyes. I must have dozed off.

Mother Jordan smiled. "Katie, I didn't mean to wake you. You looked so peaceful. You must be very tired taking care of me like this. I'm sorry."

I took her hand. "I've been worried about you. I'm the one that's sorry."

"Nonsense, you have every right to want to be courted and to get married." She stopped and took a deep breath.

"As I said, I've behaved badly. I shouldn't have—When Mr. Eberle told me he wanted to court you, I panicked. I didn't want to hear it. I wanted to get as far away as possible. You're all I have left. Forgive me, but I thought, or rather, I wanted it to be me and you forever."

"Mother Jordan, I didn't know."

"How could you know? We've never discussed anything other than living from day to day, working, and just making it through to the next year. I want you to know I love you, Katie." She patted my hand. "I do want the best for you. Really, I do. And if Mr. Eberle loves you and wants to marry you, then that is what I want for you, too."

Tears slid down my cheeks. "Thank you, but I could never leave you. You're my mother. I want to take care of you."

"That's nice, dear. But once you get married, you belong with your husband. Now hush, no more talk about me. When is your beau supposed to return?" She smiled and rubbed my hand. "I'd like to have a second introduction."

Peace moved through me. Mother Jordan gave Mr. Eberle permission to court me. The thought of that made me tingle with excitement. I couldn't wait for him to return.

Ginger and Delia returned to work that night. They couldn't afford to take any more time away from the saloon. I could take care of Mother Jordan now that she was awake.

I moved Mother Jordan into my room, so Delia could have her room back. I knew she'd be tired when she came home in the early morning hours. Mother Jordan didn't want to take my bed, but I finally convinced her I'd make a pallet on the floor. That way, I'd be close by in case she needed anything.

When Mother Jordan told me how she felt about Mr.

Eberle, the heavy cloud hanging over me melted away. I peeled potatoes to fry for Miss Ginger's girls and put the biscuits in the oven. The pot of green beans and ham boiled on the stove. It felt good to be busy in my kitchen, and hard to keep from singing when I heated water for tea. I even made Mother Jordan's favorite butter cookies to go with her tea. As the sun went down, the house grew quiet; Mother Jordan and I sat drinking tea and eating our rich cookies. Every now and then we remarked about the family-- funny times, happy times, avoiding the sad ones.

• • •

For the next three months, Mr. Eberle visited me regularly at Miss Ginger's house. When I fixed breakfast for Ginger and Delia, he was there. His presence lifted me throughout the day. I couldn't wait for his return in the evening.

Miss Delia even stopped coming in the evening for the girl's dinner. Mr. Eberle picked up that chore. "Just something to do to help out," he said.

Over breakfast one day, Miss Ginger said, "I know you two should have a chaperone while you are courting, but..." She sipped her tea. "I think we can forgo that. I'm sure Mrs. Jordan would agree. Mr. Eberle is helping to bring our dinners to us, so again, I'm confident all is well here." She smiled. "You won't let us down now, will you?"

I blushed and looked at Mr. Probus sideways. "You can trust us to be alone, Ginger."

"Ja, Ja. Trust is gut." Probus slapped his knee and nodded.

Probus and I decided to go on a picnic one afternoon. While I placed our meal of leftover fried chicken, biscuits, and pickles in the basket, Probus said he would fix the loose hinges on the screen door. When I finished, I watched him as he carefully worked his magic with the door. I wondered if I'd ever get tired of watching him work.

We rode out for about a half hour and found the perfect picnic spot—not too far from a small pond surrounded by plenty of trees. Probus spread our blanket under the biggest tree with the most shade, and I opened the basket. We ate in silence, watching the birds fly in and around the tree branches, calling to each other. It looked like they were playing a child's game of tag. A slight breeze blew the trees back and forth, their leaves swayed to the tunes of the birds.

With our stomachs full, we laid down on the blanket, each in our own thoughts, until I caught something moving beside me. I sat up quickly to see a small snake slither away. Probus jumped up, tripped, and ran to catch it. It moved much too fast for him. I started laughing. He turned and laughed, too.

"My warrior. How fast you are." I continued laughing, thinking how funny he looked when he jumped up so quickly, tripped, and tried to catch that snake. "I am sure he was harmless."

"You laugh, yet you call me a warrior?"

"Oh yes, my warrior. You reminded me of my older brother when he tried to chase a raccoon." I laughed harder. "He tripped over his feet and went end over end. His bow went one way, and he went the other."

Probus fell down beside me. "Tell me, mein Schatz, did he kill the raccoon?" He took my face in his hands.

I looked into his eyes. "No, he did not." My heart beat faster. The butterflies fluttered. "But he did get a few cuts and scrapes. He was my warrior, defending me when he needed to. Always taking care of me."

With his finger, Probus gingerly traced my eyes then ran his finger across my lips. I shivered inside. He leaned forward and kissed me. Tenderly. Goosebumps ran up and down my arms.

"Am I still your warrior?"

My throat felt dry. I could barely whisper, "Yes. You are my warrior. Mine."

Chapter 32

Christmas 1850

With Ginger and Delia sitting in the parlor, Probus helped me fix the evening meal. He wanted to show me how his mother fixed his favorite dish, German fried potatoes. I must admit, even though we didn't have all the right spices, they tasted delicious, and not too different from how Mother Jordan taught me her way to fix fried potatoes. Mother Jordan used salt and pepper, but not cinnamon. I wondered if her mother was German. After dinner, Probus helped me clean the kitchen.

I handed him a plate. He threw the towel over his shoulder and fell to the floor on one knee. "Mein Schatz," he said, taking my hand, "even though we've only been courting for three months, I feel like I know you my whole life. It's time we married." He said smiling.

I stood frozen. Even though I'll never forget the day Probus said he wanted to court me, this night was even more special. I didn't know how long a couple should court, but three months sounded fine to me. After all, I knew how to take care of a house, I could plow, plant, and harvest like any man. Isn't that what a man wanted when he got married? I felt a fondness for Probus; his presence made me feel all warm inside. And my stomach always did a little tumbling act. Wasn't that love? Now that I think about it, no one ever said how you should feel when you love someone.

"Katie, did you hear me?" Probus said.

"What?" I turned to see Ginger, Delia, and Probus smiling at me. Probus took the dish from me and steered me to the table. He pulled the chair out and gently pushed me down. Something was going on, but I couldn't put my finger on it.

"Katie, it's time we married. In my country, we court for long time, but here in America, it's different. No?" He cleared his throat. "My friend say when you meet right girl you get married. I meet right girl, and I know it right time."

I sat looking up at his face. From behind him, I heard giggles. I leaned to the side and saw Ginger and Delia, both smiling from ear-to-ear. The only one missing was Mother Jordan. "Oh my goodness, Mother Jordan. I have to tell her."

"So, you say, yes?" Probus said.

"Yes...yes, of course, yes."

Probus pulled me up and we hugged. "We'll both go see Mother Jordan tomorrow. Mr. Klingman said I take a day to do what I need to do. To take care of business, as you say."

"There's so much to do." Ginger clapped her hands, and then her hand flew to her mouth. "I'm sorry, I didn't mean to butt in, but there really is so much to do."

"I couldn't impose on you anymore. You've already done so much," I stammered. "I really must tell my mother first."

"Of course, my dear. I didn't mean to cut in. I'm just so excited for you." Ginger said as she hugged me. "For both of you."

Delia left the room without saying a word. Sometimes I felt like I walked on eggs when I was around her. She never said anything to hurt my feelings, but...she never said anything, only scowled a lot and followed Miss Ginger around taking care of her. I wondered why she never married. She was pretty enough, except for deep lines around her eyes and mouth. I saw men look at her plenty, but she never encouraged them.

"Probus, I have to go out and talk to my mother. I know she has come to accept you and me, but I must let her make plans, too."

"Of course, mein Schatz, of course. Tomorrow we go." He kissed me on the forehead and rubbed the top of my head like he always did after he kissed me.

Why does he always rub my head like that? I could feel my face turn red. "Miss Ginger, is it..."

"Yes, yes. You two do what you need to do. Delia and I will take care of things here till you get back."

Delia returned to the living room smiling and handed me a folded cloth. "I've been saving this for you. I hope you like it." She stepped back and put her hands behind her back. Her face looked softer.

"Thank you," I unfolded it to see a beautiful crocheted red shawl. I started to cry. "I saw you working on this. Wasn't it for you to keep warm during the cold months? I can't take this. You worked very hard—"

"No, I want you to have it. You've been very kind to Ginger and me—and the girls. I must not forget the girls. It's the least I can do for you. Please take it."

I hugged her. "It's beautiful, and so soft. Thank you."

It was late when Probus said good night and everyone

went to bed.

Tomorrow, we'd travel to the farm and Mother Jordan. Oh, Mother Jordan, I do love you so.

. . .

The next morning I heard a wagon pull up in front of the house before the sun rose. I threw my housecoat on and headed to the door. Probus met me as I opened it, leaned in and kissed me on the forehead.

"You must be very eager to see Mother Jordan today."

"As a matter of fact, mein Schatz, I am." He took my hands and pulled me to him. "I'm anxious to meet with your mother today." He gave me a big hug almost cutting off my air.

I pushed him back. "Well, you must let me get dressed and fix some breakfast before we leave. Miss Ginger and Delia are still asleep." I shushed him with my finger on my lips. "Please be quiet."

He started to laugh and covered his mouth with his hands. His eyes twinkled and he nodded. "Yes, yes. Quiet."

A light breakfast of biscuits and jam filled our stomachs. This morning Probus asked for coffee instead of tea, so coffee it was. I was giddy with excitement to tell Mother the news. It was too hard to keep quiet with our playful giggling and antics. Miss Ginger and Delia appeared in the doorway, all smiles.

"I see the both of you are up and ready to go," Ginger said. "That coffee really smells good; may we have a cup with you before you leave?" She sat down. "And perhaps a biscuit, too."

Delia followed suit. "We wouldn't let you leave without seeing you off and saying goodbye."

I stood up and headed to the kitchen to warm the coffee. All I could think of was our trip to the farm and telling Mother of our plans.

Today the ride out to the farm went faster than usual. I sat close to Probus and felt the strong muscles in his arms as they held the reins. Every time his body touched mine, I felt all warm and jittery inside.

Mother Jordan must have known we were coming, premonition she called it, because she stood outside the cabin when we pulled to a stop. "Good morning, my children," she said. "What brings you out here so early?"

I jumped from the wagon as soon as it came to a stop. "Mother Jordan, we have good news. I think it's good news...we want to get married very soon...I mean really soon..." I rambled.

Probus lingered while tying the horse to the post, then walked over to Mother Jordan giving her a hug. "Muttie, may I call you, Muttie?"

I stopped in my tracks. *Oh, no, how is Mother Jordan going to take to him calling her that name?* "Probus, what did you call her?"

He blushed. "Oh, I—"

Mother Jordan smiled. "I haven't heard that name in so many years. My grandfather called my grandmother, 'Muttie.' My grandfather came from the old country. He loved my grandmother very much. That was his endearing name for my grandmother."

"I didn't mean to be disrespectful Frau Jordan," he said. "I just thought that when we marry you will be my Muttie-in-law. I wanted to shorten it to Muttie."

Mother Jordan gave him a hug. "Son, you may call me 'Muttie.' I would be honored."

With a sigh of relief, I found his hand and slowly put my hand in his. "Mother Jordan, can we go inside and talk?"

She took my other hand and pulled me along. Once inside she put a pot of water on to heat for coffee. "I'll have a pot of coffee brewing in no time at all. Have a seat so we can talk."

I looked at Probus then to Mother. "Probus asked me to marry him sooner than we had talked about before." I paused. "We've come out to let you know we want to marry in a month. Do you think that would be all right?"

"And Frau Jordan," Probus interrupted, "my boss, Mr. Klingman gave me a small section of land where we can build a house." He cleared his throat. "He tells me I am one of his best hands, ja, ja, so he says build a house and start your family, too."

Mother Jordan poured the coffee. "For some reason I thought you might want to do that. Again, premonition. My mother always said I had the knack to know what was going to happen before it happened. Sometimes I wished I didn't have it." She stopped, stared at the fireplace for a moment. "Anyway, I don't see why not. I mean, yes, you can marry sooner." She clapped her hands. "Oh, my goodness, we have so much to do. And a new house to live in, too. I can be at peace knowing you are going to take good care of my Katie." She smiled and reached for my hand.

I finally breathed not realizing I had been holding my breath waiting for her answer. I stood and gave her a hug. "Thank you, Mother Jordan. Thank you."

"Yes, Muttie, thank you. I wouldn't want to marry Katie without your blessings."

Mother Jordan laughed softly. "Son, you have my blessings. I can see you love her and will take good care of her. Father Jordan would also be pleased."

With the mention of Father Jordan, tears welled in my eyes. "Mother Jordan, I'll have to get busy and make a dress. That is if we already have material."

"Katie," Mother Jordan chimed, "I think I have the perfect dress for you." She got up and headed to her bedroom.

I wondered what dress she could be talking about. When Amanda married, she made a beautiful white silk dress with lace sewn on it, a high button collar, pointed sleeves, and a long train touching the floor. Elsie's dress was a simple white dress with long sleeves and an open bodice with lace. I thought about my mother and the dress she might have worn when she married my father. The door opened.

Mother Jordan entered the room holding a blanket. She laid it on the table and unfolded it revealing a white lace dress. She beamed. "I think this may fit you. If not we can make adjustments."

I picked it up and held the dress up to me. It had a high collar almost like Amanda's and long sleeves like Elsie's dress. "Whose dress is this?"

"It was mine," Mother Jordan said. "I think Father would like you to wear it, too."

I smoothed the front of it. "Can I try it on?"

She looked at Probus. "Young man, you may go outside and check on the animals. Or, do something. We are going to try on the wedding dress." Her voice sang with merriment. "And, you do not need to see her in it until the wedding ceremony. Now, run along."

Probus got up and followed Mother Jordan's instructions, but not before kissing me on the forehead and rumpling my hair. I giggled.

Mother helped me slide the dress over my head; she fastened it down the back.

"The dress fits perfectly," Mother Jordan said. "I can't believe I was that small once. Oh what the years have done to me. But, I would not trade it for anything. I'm richly blessed, I am."

The dress had a slight flare when I twirled. I noticed the toes of my worn moccasins peeking out below the skirt. "It's beautiful. I feel like an Indian princess."

"You look like an Indian princess. Your mother would be proud of you. You are beautiful." She said giving me a hug.

Chapter 33

January 1851

The month sped by quickly. Mother Jordan arrived at Ginger's a couple of days before the wedding. Miss Ginger and Delia invited all the working girls, Mr. Goodnight and his wife, the town preacher, Matthew, Mr. Kingman and his wife, and a couple of ranch hands to be our guests.

Tables made of plywood and saw horses were placed outside and covered with tablecloths. One table held homemade breads, fried chicken, fried potatoes, and a big pot of beans. Another table held a large bowl filled with punch and a wedding cake made by the baker in town. On each end of the table set several plates of cookies.

I hadn't seen Probus since the day before. Mother Jordan said it was bad luck to see the groom on the wedding day before the wedding. The ceremony was set for one o'clock in the afternoon. By noon, several people had arrived. Ginger moved the furniture around in the living room to make room for additional chairs. Mother Jordan helped me into my dress after putting me in a vise she called a corset. She said it made the dress fit better. She tightened it so much I thought I'd faint. Then she kept me hidden away in my room. I sat on my bed as she combed and re-combed my hair.

"I want it to be perfect for you, as it should be."

A wagon pulled up in front. Without thinking, I jumped up to see who it was as Mother began pinning my hair. "Ouch."

"Oh, goodness, my girl. Sit down and let me finish."

I peered out the window, but I couldn't see who it was. Mother Jordan decided to go out and check on the guests. She was gone longer than I thought she should be. I wanted to peek out the curtain to see for myself. Just as I started to open the curtain, Mother Jordan, Amanda, and Elsie rushed into my bedroom and surrounded me.

"I didn't think...oh my goodness...how...I don't know what to say," I stammered.

"Just say you're glad to see us," Amanda said.

"I'm glad to see you." I hugged them both. "Who else is here?"

"Just us," Elsie said, "Or rather, Hayden drove us. Phoebe had to stay home with two sick children. But, we are here and we couldn't let you get married without us at your side."

Mother Jordan looked teary-eyed. "When I told the girls you were getting married, they insisted on coming. But, right now, it's almost time for you to make your appearance." She hugged me tight. "I love you, Katie. You'll be a good wife."

Elsie handed me a brown paper sack. "This is a gift for your wedding day from Hayden and Phoebe."

I slowly unwrapped the package and saw a brand new pair of white moccasins. *Hayden knows I love white moccasins.* With tears in my eyes, I whispered, "Oh, thank you, Elsie. They are a very special gift. I can't wait to thank

Hayden."

Mother Jordan and Elsie left to find their chairs in the living room. Amanda lingered behind.

She cleared her throat. "Katie, this is hard for me to say. But say it, I must." She paused. "I know I haven't always been nice to you, especially when you first came to live with us. I remember the times I kicked you out of the bed we shared, or pulled the blanket out from under you when Father told you to sit down next to me. That was not being Christian. Mother reminded me of it often." Amanda took my hand and faced me. "I want you to know I am sorry for being mean to you all those times. You've been a blessing to our family, to Mother, especially to Father. His eyes lit up each time you walked into the room. I see it now; I was jealous. I guess I had to grow up myself to be able to see it. Anyway, I wish you both many happy years together." She kissed me and turned to leave; stopping at the door, she faced me again. "And, by the way, Mother's wedding dress looks beautiful on you. It was made for you."

Before I could answer, she smiled and left.

It was time. I heard someone playing a soft melody on the fiddle. I pulled the curtain aside and slowly walked to the kitchen door leading to the living room. I could feel myself smiling. Everyone, including Amanda is happy for me. *Maybe it's as she said; she's grown up.*

Across the living room stood Probus next to the preacher, grinning from ear to ear. He looked handsome in his four-button suit, bow tie, and white shirt. His dark hair was slicked back except for that one stray lock that he couldn't control that invariably hung over his right eyebrow. My heart danced looking at him.

Mother Jordan smiled when I looked in her direction.

Amanda and Elsie held each other's hands and beamed.

Hayden winked. My emotions were overwhelming. I felt like I couldn't hold any more happiness or I would bust.

Each step I took inched me closer to my beloved. My feet felt like they were floating. I couldn't take my eyes off Probus. One foot in front of the other just like Mother Jordan taught me. "Don't rush, slowly," she had said. "Let him look at you; burn the moment in his mind, so he'll never forget." I reached Probus and the preacher. The music stopped.

I couldn't take my eyes off Probus. I couldn't tell you what either one of us said during the ceremony. I'm sure we both said we take each other for better or worse, that we would cherish each other till death. My mind raced ahead to the end when Probus would kiss me. Really, kiss me. Not a kiss on the forehead like he always did, but a deep lasting kiss, so that I wanted more.

And kiss me, he did. I smiled. This was the beginning of all my dreams coming true.

Chapter 34

1916

Grandma stood up and walked to the fireplace. I watched as she threw another log on the fire. She stoked the smoldering remains until the fire burst into new flames. Once again, she sat down and quietly stared straight ahead. I crawled back up on her lap and got comfortable. She took deep shallow breaths; I thought she might have fallen asleep. It was quiet except for the popping of embers. I nudged her. "Grandma?"

She coughed slightly. "Oh, yes, where was I?"

"You married Grandpa. Was it really your dream come true?"

She sat straighter in the rocker and smiled. "Yes, my little butterfly. It was. There were some rough times, just like any family, but, all in all, Papa was still my warrior. I did grow to love him very much. It was a love built on helping each other face one day at a time, respecting our private times, and coming together when one of us needed lifting up when we felt low."

I giggled imagining my grandfather wearing a breach cloth. "What happened to Miss Ginger? And..."

Grandma chuckled. "As Papa would say, ja, ja, you are

full of questions, mein Schatz. He called me his Schatz a lot."

"What does that mean? Was it German?"

"Yes, it was his native language, German. It means sweetheart. I was his sweetheart. I can still see him smiling with that unruly lock of hair bobbing from his forehead. I loved running my fingers through it. Oh, my, listen to me. Like a love sick young girl."

"But, Grandma…"

"Now child, it's getting late, but I will tell you this. All six of our children turned out to be good, upstanding, people. True, some of the boys got a little rambunctious at times, but they married and graced us with many grandchildren. Grandchildren just like you, dear one." She leaned back in her rocker and pulled me closer to her. "Mother Jordan lived a long life and I was able to be with her the day she passed on. I'll never forget the sweet look on her face the day we buried her. She knew she would see her Father she read about in her Good Book. Perhaps she was also thinking about seeing Father Jordan again."

"But what about Miss Ginger, and what about your sisters? Did you ever see them again?"

She patted my leg. "Well, Ginger stayed on at the saloon for probably ten more years before a wealthy gentleman from the east came to town. He swept her off her feet, so to speak. They married and moved back east. And, yes, Delia went with her. They'd been together so long it was just natural they'd stay together. I lost touch with her after she left." Grandma had that faraway look once more.

"Grandma, are you thinking of your sisters? Where did they go?"

"I never saw my sisters again. I heard the riverboat

took them to St. Louis and from there they were sent to reservations. Some went to Kansas, Iowa, and others went to Oklahoma." She sighed lightly.

I leaned my head against Grandma's shoulder. I wished I could stay here forever feeling the warmth of her body and the light fragrance of honeysuckle on her neck. Her story of survival and perseverance made me feel so proud of her.

. . .

Afterword

Note from the Author

Catherine Clare Jordan, also known as Katie, and Kate Eberle, did survive the Black Hawk War and married Probus Eberle, of German decent and together they raised six children. I became deeply involved with Katie in my quest to find my own ancestors.

From my mother's divorce papers, I discovered she had an affair with a man by the name of Bud Wyburn and from that union there was a child. The papers stated the child was born on my birthdate. I immediately started searching for his family. It took me almost seven years with many letters written and meeting new relatives. Through DNA, I learned Wyburn was not my father. DNA doesn't lie.

Bud Wyburn was the great grandson of Katie. By the time I found out I was not related, I was too deeply enthralled with her life and her story. I felt I needed to be her voice and tell her story. I do hope I've done her justice. I still feel a kinship with her even though I'm not related. I tried to stay with what Katie said during her interview with a journalist. Of course, a lot about Katie's life had to be created as best I could. I'd like to think the way I've portrayed it, it could have happened.

There are many stories of children surviving wars, women who helped behind enemy lines, and men saving the lives of their fallen comrades. I hope I have done honor to this one.

There remains so much more to Indian Kate's story. Kate's given name by Thomas Jordan was Catherine Clare

Jordan. Kate is buried in the East Dubuque cemetery in East Dubuque, Illinois. At this time, she does not have a headstone. There is a movement between a great, great, granddaughter and the Sac Council to have a stone placed there for her. It has been a long process, lots of paperwork, and waiting.

There are numerous newspaper articles written about Indian Kate Eberle; articles concerning the money she received from the government since she did not live on the reservation, the article about her son William when he tried to commit suicide, and where she was living at the time of her death. The state of Wisconsin has articles written about the Black Hawk War.

Katie's story was the vision I saw when I read the following newspaper article in the Dubuque Times dated Jan 9, 1892.

The Dubuque Times

Dubuque, IA
Saturday Evening, Jan 9, 1892

BLACKHAWK HER CHIEF—The Rough Adventures of an Indian Girl

Now a resident of East Dubuque separated from her family at the time of battle of Bad Axe. Adopted by Farmer Jordan, she has seen Dubuque grow from two or three log cabins to the city of today.

The story of the suffering and danger through which the few white settlers in this vicinity passed during the Black Hawk war in 1832 has often been told in the memories of some of the older readers of *The Times* it forms a never fading picture. But of the privations of the band who followed Black Hawk in his flight toward the Mississippi, the starving warriors with their squaws and papooses, who overtaken at the mouth of the Bad Axe and almost exterminated in that final battle less has been known to the reading public.

One of that band of Indians is now living in East Dubuque and the story of her life is given in her own words below.

In answer to the Times reporter questions Mrs. Eberle who is a dignified woman nearing three score and ten, erect, active and with jet-black hair slightly tinged with grey said, "As far back as I can remember I lived with my father and mother and sisters and brothers in our wigwam. There was a string of wigwams there but I don't know where the place was. We used to move around—we didn't always live in one place. The wigwams had a fire on the ground and the smoke went out at the top. They had puckways built up about so high (3 or 4 feet) around them.

"What are puckways?"

"They were made out of weeds and grass to keep the wind out.

The Indians used to raise corn."

"How did they prepare the ground?"

"They made a flat paddle out of wood and dug it up. A lot of them would work together and dig the ground up and then make a fence of poles around it to keep everything away. Our chief, you know he was Black Hawk. Well, I remember when he came to what's that they do when they make soldiers?"

"Drill?"

"Yes, he came to drill them and they had tomahawks and guns to fight with. Well the first thing you know they was gone to fight."

"Next thing Black Hawk came again and they took the horses and women and children, and the children they put on the horses with the big packs and then we started and went through swamps till you'd think we'd all fall off. We children didn't think of danger— wasn't old enough, but we got very hungry."

"Well, we'd traveled a long time—a good many days—we came to the river and we all stopped to cook something. You bet we was hungry. Between sundown and dark that same evening Black Hawk had his men all on the ridge above the river and the white men came and began the battle. Then my mother gave me to my sister and my aunt and they took me in a canoe. Well, we got in a canoe the three of us."

"Was it a birch bark or a log canoe?"

"I don't know, couldn't tell you, sir. Well so we got in and there was a kind of a sand island and we had a little river to cross. Well, while we was going across that river there come the shooting, it was dark and the bullets went whizzing! It seemed as though there was thousands and thousands. We went across on the sand island and we stayed there till next evening. We had left the canoe to get away from the bullets and we had …

"How many children had your mother?"

"As well as I can remember there was three girls of us and four brothers. Well, when we got across the river we went I don't know how far. We went and we traveled until we got perished and we traveled until we got done out. I couldn't walk any more then one would carry me on her back and then the other one would. Then we came to a kind of a prairie of grass and then they both laid down and they wrapped me up in the blanket and you know when a child is tuckered out she'll just lay down and sleep, and I don't know how long I slept and when I waked up I was all alone and I looked all around and I couldn't see nobody.

"I had sense enough to know which way we come in…you know there's this high prairie grass and whenever you make a trail you can see it. Well, I took the back trail—I couldn't see no trail no other way and I went back to the river."

"When I got to the edge of the river it was dark; it was so dark that I couldn't see to get no farther. I set myself down against a big tree. I set myself down and laid on my side and went to sleep and once in the night I waked up and I couldn't hear nothing but these big owls."

"You were not afraid of them, were you?"

"No, I wasn't afraid of nothing, then."

"But didn't you feel very lonely and miss your mother and father and brothers and sisters?"

"Oh, yes, of course. And then I turned over on the other side and I slept there until morning."

"You'll never forget how you felt at that time, will you, Mrs. Eberle?"

"Oh, no, never, never, never. No one knows what starvation is till they have to go through it."

"Well, next morning I went down to the river to get a drink."

"Had you no water the day before?"

"No, nor nothing at all to eat. Well, I was goin' down along the riverbank and you know what a noise it makes when you're trampin' in the leaves and brush. Well, as I was goin' down an Indian man, he come along behind me and I looked over my shoulder this way, and he had on a white man's shirt and so I thought he was a white man. I had never seen an Indian wear white man's clothes. The Indian men wore breechclouts and leggings and moccasins and I had never seen any white man that I can remember or expecting in the boat. So I ran away as fast as I could and I tripped and fell and then he hollered at me. Of course I knew our language then and I wasn't afraid."

"Do you know any Indian words now?"

"Oh, very few. The Indian man was awful glad to have company. He took me with him and after while I got so weak I couldn't carry my heavy blanket anymore and then he took the blanket and put the shirt on me."

"You had kept your blanket with you?"

"Oh, yes indeed. I stuck to that. I didn't have any other clothes. We went along down the river and we didn't have nothing to eat but roots and bark and such things as we could find in the woods, and after awhile we saw some bark canoes on the other side of the river so the Indian made a little raft and put me on it and we went over and he picked out the best one and then we come down the river in that, and he got a lot of soft maple bark and that was the last thing we had to eat till we got here."

"When we were coming down the river we seen a big keel boat that was sent to gather up the prisoners and we jumped out and pulled up our boat and threw brush and leaves over it so they couldn't see it and then we went up behind some big trees till the boat got out of sight. Then we got in the boat and never got out till we got here, then our little boat leaked so that we had to get out. At this place where East Dubuque is covered with heavy lumber and there was no house but Father Jordan's and where Dubuque is was heavy timber too and there were no houses there but three or four log cabins."

"All this was full of those big large willows and there was what they call the fall grapes on them and we got out to get the grapes and Father Jordan came up to me. I said Kookush and Quasheean while holding up the grapes.

"What do they mean?"

"Pigmeat and bread."

"Did he understand them?"

"Oh, yes, he knew some of the Indian words. Some friendly Indians used to come here. The boys coaxed the Indian to come down and they took us to the house and he had eleven bullet wounds in his neck and face and he told them, that, we had been eleven days and nights without anything to eat, only what we could pick up."

"They thought he was my brother and they kept him two weeks and then they took him to Galena but they kept me with them."

"Were they always good to you?"

"Oh, my, yes. And Mother Jordan had thirteen children of her own and lived to see them all grown up and married and outlived all but four of them. She lived to see her grandchildren, and great-great-grandchildren. Mother Jordan said that she could always say that she raised fifteen children. She was a hundred and eleven years old when she died."

"How long did Mr. Jordan live after you came there?"

"About two years. And the last thing he said on his dying bed he put out his hand to Mother Jordan and said: Mary Ann, take good care of Katie."

"They always called me Katie."

"What was your Indian name?"

"I don't know our family name. My first name was Sop-ho-kab, my youngest brother's Si-o-noh and my mother's Kat-e-quah. I don't remember the names of the others."

"Did you ever see any of them again?"

"Only once. When the keel boat came back it had about three hundred prisoners and it stopped here and the captain asked Father Jordan to bring me down to see if I had any relations on the boat and my oldest sister and one of my aunts were there and they knew me. They were not the ones who took me away from the battle, but a married sister who did not live with us and another aunt. The captain said they could go up to the house and stay with me until the boat started and they came. The boat stopped for provisions— the prisoners were almost starved. Father Jordan gave them three beeves and they butchered them there."

"Did he have many cattle?"

"Yes, I think he had a hundred or more. And when the captain asked him how much he charged for the cattle he said nothing and that those poor, starving Indians could have two or three more if they wanted them."

"Mother Jordan thought I was about seven years old because I was just beginning to lose my front teeth and her children had begun to lose their teeth when they were about seven years old."

"Did you live with Mrs. Jordan until you were married?"

"When I grew to be a young woman I went out to work for other people. Mother Jordan cried like everything when I first went away to work. She said 'Oh, Katie if Pap was alive, you wouldn't have to do it.'"

During the interview, a fine-looking young man came in whom Mrs. Eberle introduced as her youngest son, William.

Besides this son, who is twenty-one years of age, Mrs. Eberle has two older sons, John and William, both of whom are married and live in East Dubuque. Her husband, Probus Eberle, a well-known German farmer of East Dubuque, died a few years ago. She has also three daughters.

Mrs. Eberle says that in 1832 Mr. Jordan was running a ferryboat between his home and Dubuque. It was a flat boat propelled by two rowers on each side and steered by Mr. Jordan. After his death, Mrs. Jordan got a horse ferryboat, which was run for some time. Mr. Jordan and two of his sons were buried on the hill above East Dubuque. The old well, which was near their house could be seen in the middle of the principal street until a few years ago, when it was either filled up or covered over. When their land was sold, each of the children received as his share twelve hundred dollars.

This newspaper article came from the Cunningham Museum in Lancaster, Wisconson.